Eggnog And Whiskey

A Brother's Best Friend Holiday Romance

Sierra Shipley

Copyright

Table of Contents

Books By Sierra

The Claiming Her Series
His Temptation
His Disaster
His Reward
His Challenge

The Rose Prairie Series
All books in The Rose Prairie Series are standalone set in the small town of Rose Prairie.
All Tangled Up
Tied In Nots
It Had To Be You

Interconnected Stand-Alone
Yes, Captain
Hey, Neighbor

The Single Dads Club
Loved by the Single Dad
Nanny for the Single Dad
Desired by the Single Dad

Chapter One

Danielle

Christmas music plays through the sound system, lost in the drone of holiday shoppers. Apparently, we're all fed up with hearing "*I Want a Hippopotamus For Christmas*," content to ignore the catchy tune in favor of stocking stuffers.

If it were up to me, I'd be back at my apartment cuddled up with Felix, pre-gaming the annual downward spiral into the pit of loneliness and despair.

It's the most wonderful time of the year.

"Yeah, I just don't know if he'll like it." Lindsay purses her lips at the little toy excavator. The yellow truck clicks against its cardboard box as she examines it, as if changing the angle will help her decide.

Last-minute Christmas shopping is our tried-and-true tradition. She kidnaps and drags me from department store to department store in search of the perfect gifts. I know she does it to keep my mind occupied, which I love her for, but I wish she'd be more decisive.

People pass by bundled in winter coats and scarves, their carts full as they rush to finish their Christmas shopping. It's chaos, but the familiarity of it all fills me with nostalgia.

"Your nephew's five. I doubt he's going to care all that much." My best friend chews her lip, eyes dancing between me and the toy. "He'll play with it for like three seconds before it's tossed in the corner, and in four months your sister-in-law will donate it to Goodwill or something."

Lindsay rolls her eyes at me, trying to suppress a smile. She knows I'm right, but she won't admit it. "Nick's really into this stuff."

"Then buy it." I soften my tone and reach for the toy. "It's the thought behind the gift that counts, and I'm sure he's gonna love it. What kid wouldn't want to dig around in the dirt with that thing?"

"Alright." She relents, giving me the toy to place in the gradually growing cart.

This is how our shopping always goes. Lindsay finds an item she likes, second-guesses herself, and puts it back on the shelf only to come back for it five minutes later. I think she drags me here to convince her to buy things. Otherwise, she'd never get her Christmas shopping done.

"Where are we off to next?" I grab the cart, following her through the store as Lindsay checks her list.

By the time I've convinced her to buy the gifts she originally set out to get, we stop at a restaurant for dinner. The Italian bistro smells of garlic and freshly baked bread that has my mouth watering.

"Italian was a good call. I'm starving." Cool air caresses my neck as I unwind the thick scarf. The gold necklace around my neck sways with each scooch into the booth. Warm metal settles into my palm, the letter zinging along the chain out of habit. Both the booth and the chain are a tad bit tighter than they used to be, but grief affects us all differently. Mine added a few pounds to my ass, tits, and tummy, but instead of fighting it, I'm embracing my newly formed curves.

"Mm-hmm," Lindsay agrees around a bite of steaming breadstick, motioning for me to grab one.

We both eat far too many breadsticks, and by the time our food arrives, I don't know if I can eat another bite.

"Are you coming tomorrow?" Lindsay asks, swirling spaghetti around her fork. Her wide blue eyes are soft and pleading, and full of hope.

4

For years, she's invited me to spend the Christmas holiday with her family. They eat a large feast before driving around the city to look at Christmas lights.

"Ah, so that's what today has been about," I tease, brushing my long brown hair over my shoulder to keep it from getting covered in Alfredo sauce. "How long have you been wanting to ask me?"

"Shut up," she laughs. "But really, are you going to come? I promise it won't be weird."

She's done this for the past three years and I love her for it, but nothing could get me to spend Christmas with her family. Seeing her parents and her brother, his wife and kids, it'll be too much. A reminder of everything I had and lost. So, I'd rather spend the entire holiday at home.

Alone.

"Linds," I sigh.

"Dani."

I look back down at my pasta covered in melting Parmesan cheese, swirling my fork around and around until the bite is so big I know I won't be able to talk around it, and shove it into my mouth.

Lindsay laughs as fettuccine falls back onto my plate. "You're such a child. I can't believe I can go anywhere with you."

It breaks my heart knowing I'm disappointing her. She asks out of love for me, but I can't bring myself to go. There's only so much I can take this time of year, and it all feels like too much. My fragile emotions would crack and break.

Once I've swallowed my food without choking, I reach across the table for her hand. "You know I love you, right?" Lindsay nods, her hopeful expression falling. "Staying home is best for me right now." I blink back the tears I feel building behind my eyes. Christmas Eve used to be a magical time. Happy. But now all it leaves is an aching hole in my chest. "Plus, I already have my fridge stocked with eggnog."

She smiles softly and squeezes my hand before releasing it. "You know you're always welcome, right? Don't think you can't change your mind."

"I know." I smile softly at my best friend before diving back into my pasta.

THE COMBINATION OF my oversized flannel shirt and fuzzy socks is exactly what I need right now. Snow began falling on our drive back from the restaurant, and I knew tonight called for cozy comfort. The minute the lock clicked behind me, I turned on the gas fireplace, lit the candle that smells like Christmas heaven, and changed into my pajamas.

Felix, my ash-colored cat, curls up in my lap, purring softly. Silky fur slips through my fingers, his comforting purrs rumbling against my stomach. Christmas music plays from the too-large TV hung over the mantle that Robbie insisted we buy years ago. Now, I don't think I have it in me to get rid of it.

A tiny Christmas tree twinkles in the corner, empty of presents except for one. It'll stay there until New Year's Eve, when Lindsay and I exchange gifts. It started when we were teenagers. We got it into our heads that exchanging gifts was better suited for the new year. What better way to ring in the new year than opening a present?

My thumb slides through my social media feed filled with distant relatives posting pictures of their kids, old high school friends spending a night out on the town, and an inspirational quote or two from some random account. There's no purpose in my scrolling. I don't need to see how joyful everyone is this time of year, but I can't stop myself. Seeing their happiness is my own fucked-up version of therapy.

Just as I'm about to call it quits, my phone buzzes. A banner notification pops up at the top of my screen, and I freeze.

My heart races in overdrive, and my muscles tighten as if I've been drenched in frigid water.

6

EGGNOG AND WHISKEY

Logan.

My dead brother's best friend, Logan.

Logan, the person I considered family that abandoned me the moment the aneurysm ripped my brother away, leaving me all alone with no one to call home.

Logan, the guy who didn't attend his best friend's funeral. His family showed up, but he didn't. They were there for me, but I needed *him,* and he was nowhere to be found.

The screen blurs as my vision fades. Shock, bone-deep, rolls through me. My mind races, but my body hangs in limbo.

Three years.

Three years with no word, no contact, not even a fucking postcard, and now he wants to reach out?

Seconds drag into minutes. The notification slips away unopened.

Shock rolls into anger, bitter and biting. As if it's lava, I toss my phone on the end of the couch, leaving the message unread.

Felix looks up at me, his yellow eyes blinking. "Sorry, bud, but I have to get up." He issues a grumbling complaint when I lift him off my lap.

My bare thighs are cold without the weight of the blanket or Felix's warm body, but I have to get rid of this tension I feel being pulled tight under my skin. The hardwood floor echoes with each stomp of my foot as I pace in front of the fireplace.

"The audacity of this man to reach out to me a day before Christmas Eve. He's the only other person who knows what it's like to have lost my brother, and he picks now—the holiday that meant the most to us—to make contact? Logan was always there, always right beside Robbie and me for everything. He was our found family, and he abandoned me."

Felix's little head turns from side to side as he watches me pace, his ears twitching as I talk to him. He might not talk back, but I'm pretty sure he can sense the frustration in my tone.

"I should ignore it, right? Say 'fuck you' and not open it. Let him see how it feels when someone ignores you." Felix twitches his tail against the couch cushion. "But what if I open it and leave it on read? It might hurt worse to know I read it and chose not to respond."

Decision made, I dart back to the couch and dig through the blanket until I find my phone. I open the app and click back into my inbox. My eyes snag on the thumbnail of Logan's picture like it's the first time I've seen it. It's one of him and Robbie as teenagers, flexing their arms, cocky looks on their faces on the top of some big rock they climbed.

With a heavy exhale, I square my shoulders and click open the message.

Chapter Two

Logan

I'm such an ass. Admitting my flaws won't help with the shitstorm waiting for me.

If she texts back. And it's a big fucking if.

She's going to answer, right? Tomorrow's Christmas Eve, for fuck's sake. Our night. The night the three of us became a family. Surely we can do it again, right?

There's been a lot I've avoided in the last three years. Avoiding the only things, the only people I care about, hasn't been the best choice I've ever made. In fact, it's one of the worst. Definitely a top-three contender for the worst decisions of all time.

But it's time to face the mess I've made. Starting with Dani.

The screen time's out, and I immediately tap it back to life. If she texts me back, there's no way in hell I'm going to miss it.

For it being this close to a holiday, the hotel bar is empty. Probably because most people in town are spending their time with their family and not alone drowning their sorrows with whiskey.

I haven't been back in Chicago in three years, running from everything. Moved across the country and made every excuse I could to avoid this city and the memories that lie down every street.

The alcohol warms my chest, leaving a burn in its wake.

Dani's pissed; I know that much. It was never hard to read her, but it doesn't take a genius to know why.

Because I'm an ass.

I deserve every moment of torture coming my way. She's probably mad as hell and is going to make me squirm. And, fuck, it's working. Maybe I should've come up with a more convincing opening line.

Tapping the dimming screen, a "read" notification pops up under my text. "Come on, Dani. Answer me." My fingers rap against the tumbler, anxiously waiting for her response.

There wasn't a lot of thought behind the message. A simple "hey" was the only thing I deemed good enough to send. I hate myself for it, but what else can I say? It's not that I have nothing to say; it's that I don't know how to say it. There's not enough time in the world, and no amount of long messages will be good enough. Shit, knowing Dani, she wouldn't even read them.

The bartender comes to my end of the bar wearing his black-on-black outfit with hipster suspenders hooked to his belt loops. "Can I get you another one?" He tilts his head to the empty tumbler in my hand.

"No, thanks. I've made enough mistakes tonight. I don't need to make one more." He smiles politely, but I know he's thinking I'm crazy.

Tonight, maybe I am.

Who messages their dead best friend's little sister after three years?

I've got to be out of my fucking mind.

Damn you, Robbie.

I slide the glass over and check my phone one last time before heading up to my hotel room. My parents are more than thrilled to have me back in town, but their house is crowded. My sister Brittney and her daughter recently moved in, and my baby sister Allison just graduated college and is saving up for an apartment. Besides, I need time to process being back.

The ding of my phone is like a gunshot. It knocks me back on my heels and sends my heart racing. But it also has a smile crossing my face.

Dani: fuck you
Me: how are you?
Dani: ur an asshole

Me: I know

Me: How are you?

The Dani I know would leave this conversation here, but I hope like hell she doesn't. Maybe she's feeling like me and needs some sort of connection to Robbie.

Those three little dots torment me, bouncing tauntingly for what seems like an eternity.

Dani: how do you think?

Me: messed up. missing Robbie. like me.

Me: Can I see you tomorrow? Do some traditions. For Robbie.

There it is—the whole reason I messaged her. I'm lucky that I've even gotten this far. Thinking about her messages three years ago, full of anger and hurt lashing out at me, makes me worried about her response. What I get back isn't a raving agreement, but I'll take it.

Sure.

IT'S A FUCKING SAUNA in here. I'm not sure they'll take the suit back because I'm sweating out of every conceivable pore on my body.

People quirk their eyebrows when they see me coming, but if we're going to do traditions, I'm going all out. Plus, I think Dani will get a good laugh out of it.

I hope.

Plastic bags bounce against my thigh as I walk on the salted sidewalk to Dani's apartment. I'm not sure what she's expecting, but she's going to be in for a surprise. There haven't been any more messages since last night, so I'm hoping she hasn't already ordered food because there's enough here to feed five people.

It's been over three years since I've walked this street, and already my eyes burn uncomfortably. Everything is the same as I remember. The red-brick facade is untouched. Streetlights are still buzzing as they flicker. This place used to be so achingly familiar.

Now it's a graveyard of memories.

I reach the glass doors of the apartment building and pause. Dani might've said I could come over, but I'm still doubtful that she'll let me in.

My breath fogs in front of me as I work up the courage to buzz her apartment. For minutes, I stare at the nameplate. At Dani and Robbie's names written in his terrible scrawl, and I'm frozen, unable to push the small button.

The door clicks open, snapping me out of my stupor. I have to jump back to avoid getting smacked by the door.

An elderly lady with a cane struggles to hold the heavy door. She shoots me a thankful smile when I extend a hand to hold the door for her. Like everything else, her wrinkled face is familiar. I nod, wishing her a Merry Christmas as she passes.

Her laughter follows me up the stairs to Dani's apartment.

We were twenty-one when they sold their parents' house and moved to the apartment. Dani had just graduated from high school. Robbie had a job in a garage, and the house was sucking away what little money their parents had left them. Their aunt offered to take them both in, but Robbie refused. She lived several hours away, and his job was here, and there was no way he was going to leave Dani.

I've never seen someone grow up as quickly as Robbie did.

And then he died.

A torrent of memories flits through my head, hitting me like a punch to the gut. How many times had we stumbled up these stairs drunk off our asses after a night out? I knew tonight would be bittersweet, but nothing could've prepared me for the downpour of hurt peeling back the still unhealed wound of losing my best friend.

Who am I kidding? This is a permanent festering sore on my soul that will never heal—will never scab over and reveal a fresh scar.

It will always be as it is now: raw.

Nerves settle in as I stand on the third-floor landing in front of Dani's apartment door. The solid oak seems to taunt me with all the things I left behind when Robbie died.

Who I left behind.

There aren't expectations for how this reunion will go. She's mad as hell, and I doubt she'll let me step a foot inside. But I'll never know if I don't try.

I suck in several fortifying breaths. Here goes nothing.

My knuckles rap against the door, and I stare at the floor under my booted feet, waiting for Dani to answer it.

The door creaks open, only wide enough to peek through. Dani's face peers at me through the small crack. Her eyebrow arches as she takes me in, Santa costume and all. "Wow, I'm surprised you actually showed up. I'll admit...you committed." She snorts, shaking her head before opening the door.

But she doesn't let me in.

Instead, she blocks the doorway, her arms crossed like a soldier standing guard. Her stony gaze bounces around as she takes me in. Those hazel eyes pin me in place, flaying me open and seeing the broken man within.

I look at her too. Somehow she's gone from a girl to a woman. Her dark brown hair flows down her back, hidden behind womanly curves that weren't there before. She's always been a cute girl, but before me stands a beautiful woman. It's her eyes though, filled with sorrow, that steals my breath. That all too familiar pain lingering in their hazel depths.

It's the twin to mine. The same pain I see when I look in the mirror.

"I figured it was the only way you'd let me in the door. I was half convinced you'd keep me locked out here."

"I thought about it. Still might." Dani looks at me a moment longer, her lips pursing. Indecision flickers across her face before resignation. Maybe she senses the same warmth in her chest that I do. Dani takes a deep breath before stepping out of the doorway, and motions for me to come inside.

Every inch of this place holds a memory. The brown leather couch Robbie and I struggled to get up the steps. Their mom's spoon collection hangs next to their dad's chef's apron in the kitchen. The large TV above the fireplace. I'm amazed it's still hanging since we had no clue what we were doing. History is everywhere in this place, and I don't know whether I should laugh or cry.

I follow her into the kitchen, and set the bag of Chinese food on the counter. Emotion clogs my throat, and I clear it, trying not to sound like I'm about to lose it. "I hope you're hungry." The space is the same as I remember, but it's not like it should be. "Not much of a Christmas decorator anymore?" Dani passes behind me, reaching for plates.

"There's no point anymore. I've got the tree up, though." She angles her chin over her shoulder toward the living room and the large industrial window. One tiny tree with flickering lights rests in the corner, a lone present tucked underneath it. "Besides," she shrugs, plates clattering on the counter. "That was always a Christmas Eve thing, anyway. Thanks for the food, by the way. I'm not sure I have anything of true substance in the house."

"What were you going to eat if I hadn't shown up?"

"I've got eggnog in the fridge." She says it as if it makes complete sense. Handing me a plate, she digs through the bags. "Yes," she hisses. "You got dumplings!"

The excitement in her voice makes me chuckle. She might be grown up, but she's the same girl I knew. "Like I could forget your obsession. Robbie and I had to fight to get even one from your grubby little grasp." Dani's already shoved one into her mouth and is dumping the entire container onto her plate. "Hey, no you don't. You have to share."

My hand wraps around her small wrist. I'm more than willing to fight her for the dumpling box. Dani turns away from me, curling her body around the mostly empty box, her ass pressing against my dick as we wrestle. Like she's a live-wire, I step back, putting space between us. It seems my cock doesn't understand that she's Robbie's sister and therefore completely off-limits.

"Ha," she says victoriously before noticing I've grabbed her plate and stolen half her dumplings. "Hey, that's cheating. Here, give me my dumplings back and I'll give you the box."

"Absolutely not." I hold my plate high over her head, grab several of the boxes sitting on the counter, and dash past her into the living room. She issues a meager protest but doesn't chase after me, grabbing the remaining food boxes and the bottle of whiskey from the counter before sitting next to me.

We've somehow fallen back into our old roles. Dani and I would tease and pick on one another. Robbie was our referee, always having to step between us to keep Dani from trying to strangle me to death.

I wonder what will happen to us without him. If we'll finally tear each other apart.

Dani places the boxes on the coffee table, the glass bottle hitting the top with a thud. Fire blazes in the fireplace, warming the room as Dani picks up the remote. "Let's get this started."

Robbie and I were eighteen when their parents died in a car accident, and I wasn't going to let him and Dani go through their first Christmas without them alone. My parents have six kids, so I wasn't missed too much. I spent whatever time I could with them, and Christmas Eve was ours.

Dani finds what she's looking for. Our traditional Christmas Eve movie starts. It wasn't our finest moment when we decided that Die Hard was an acceptable thing to watch with his thirteen-year-old kid sister. We never claimed to be the most responsible eighteen-year-olds, just desperate ones.

"I almost forgot. I have something for you." Dani narrows her eyes when I take my dumpling-loaded plate to the kitchen with me. "I thought this year you could play along. There can't be a Santa without his elf."

"O-oh no," she snickers, waving her hand at me. I reach into the other plastic bag. "I am *not* changing into an elf costume. That was supposed to be you and Robbie."

"It's not the entire costume, just the ears." She eyes the small, felt-covered object I hold out to her. I stopped by a drugstore and picked up an elf ear headband, knowing she'd react like this.

"I guess that's not so bad," she relents, taking the headband from me. I hide my smile as I sit at the other end of the couch.

On our first Christmas Eve, Robbie and I dressed up as Santa and his elf. We would've done anything to keep her from being sad, so we did the most ridiculous thing we could think of. Her squeals of laughter when we stormed into her bedroom and dragged her out of bed made everything worth it. From that moment on, she insisted that every Christmas we dress up all over again.

Dani slides the ears onto her head and gives me a look that says, '*You happy now?*' God, she's gorgeous. She's always been cute, but she's different now. Strong. Resilient.

But I'm different now too.

Everything's different.

Chapter Three

Logan

Gunfire rages from the TV as *Nakatomi Plaza* gets overtaken, while Dani and I eat our food in relative silence. We sit at opposite ends of the couch, and I can't stop glancing over to where she mouths lines from the movie. The three of us used to quote the movie, laughing the whole time. Robbie knew every line, changing his voice to get us to laugh. With him, it's not the same.

A large gray cat pounces onto the back of the couch. "What the fuck?" I gasp, nearly throwing my plate of food across the room.

Dani lets out a peal of laughter so bright and warm that I melt into it. "That's Felix," she explains, reaching for the cat and pulling it into her lap.

"Why Felix? Kinda a strange name for a cat." I offer my hand for him to sniff.

She strokes a hand down the cat's side. Instantly, loud purrs rumble from him. "He's a cat. Feline. Felix. Get it?"

"No," I say with a chuckle.

"Lindsay agreed with me." She shrugs as if that changes anything. Felix allows me to pet the top of his head, and Dani's hand casually grazes against mine. "I got him shortly after Robbie died. Well, I say I got him, but really it was Lindsay. She said I needed someone to keep me company and shoved him into my arms with a bag full of kitten food and toys. He's been my little buddy ever since."

Hot, bitter shame settles in my gut. I should've been here keeping her company. I should've been here to pick up the pieces, but I wasn't. It's what Robbie would've wanted. But I couldn't deal with any of it.

"She's a good friend."

"And so are you, Felix," she says in a baby voice. The cat blinks its large yellow eyes as if to say, '*I know*' in that smug way I assume all cats think. "Wanna hand me the whiskey? I hate moving when he's purring."

"Yeah." I snag the bottle from the coffee table, twisting the top and taking a swig before handing it to Dani. She scoffs, shooting me a crooked grin before bringing the bottle to her lips.

I watch captivated as she tips her head back, the amber liquid gliding through her plump lips, throat working as she swallows it down.

What the fuck am I doing? I have got to get a hold of myself. This is ridiculous. I don't need to be watching her drink. Thinking about how soft her hand was against mine, and I certainly don't need to be picturing what those curves look like underneath all those clothes. Or how soft those lips would be wrapped around my cock.

Fuck, pull yourself together.

Thankfully, Dani's too focused on the screen to notice me trying to cover my hardening cock.

With great effort, I settle back into the couch and try to focus on John McClane being a badass, taking on terrorists who are doing a shit job at keeping everything contained.

We pass the bottle back and forth. It doesn't take long for the whiskey to make us more comfortable. I slip off my boots, tugging open the fuzzy coat. Dani sprawls on the couch, her blanket-wrapped feet resting near my thigh. We're laughing, quoting the movie like we used to. Something so simple somehow eases the ache in my chest.

This is what I needed: a sense of normalcy—as normal as it can be without Robbie.

When the movie ends, we watch the credits roll, both of us somber. "That was the first time I've watched it since Robbie died." My admission hangs heavy between us.

Dani's quiet for a moment, stroking Felix's fur before saying, "I haven't decorated for Christmas since Robbie, either. I can watch the movie, but the decorating is too much, especially when I'm all on my own."

Dani's changed in the years we've been apart. Once bright and bubbly, there's an overwhelming sadness in her eyes. Dark circles rest under them as if they've been there for some time. The things she used to enjoy doing, like decorating for Christmas, have become a hardship, which I completely understand. Aren't I in the same boat? We're both heartbroken and lonely.

So fucking lonely.

I nudge her knee. "Then let's decorate. Robbie would want us to." Felix's eyes pop open to glare at me for disturbing him. "Where are your decorations?"

Tonight's about bringing back traditions, even if it fucking hurts.

Standing, I offer my hand to her. She sighs heavily but places her hand in mine. Felix meows, jumping off the couch and disappearing. I don't think I'm making friends in the Felix department.

She sets down the half-empty bottle of whiskey. "In my bedroom, shoved under the bed somewhere." Dani crosses the room, and I follow.

Definitely don't look at her ass. Nope. Keep your eyes off her round ass. Damn it, I looked.

"Do you need help getting it?" I ask as she flips on her bedroom light.

"No, I've got it." Dani braces a hand on the bed, lowering herself to her knees.

Yeah, I'm in trouble.

It's impossible not to watch as Dani leans down, her ass in the air as she wiggles herself under the bed. The edge of her elf-ear headband bumps against the frame, pulling it back on her head.

I clear my throat. "I think I should get it."

"No, I've got it. I wouldn't want you to find something you shouldn't."

Oh, fuck. Is she...she can't mean what I think she means, right?

Shit, I've got to get my mind out of the gutter.

The stretchy fabric of her leggings is nearly see-through. Candy canes are peppered across her ass like sprinkles on a sundae. I don't know why, but seeing those little candy canes makes me chuckle.

"What?" she shouts. "Did you say something?"

I shake my head and rub a hand down my face. "I asked if you almost have it."

"Oh, yeah." Her legs kick as she pulls herself out from under the bed, her face flushed but smiling as she pulls several thin stacked tubs out from their hiding place. She taps the sides. "It's all right here. You can carry them to the living room, though. I'm happy to watch you struggle."

"Struggle? I think you've got this all wrong. These are going to be a piece of cake." On impulse, I remove my Santa coat and toss it on her bed. Red fuzzy lint covers my black undershirt, so I rake a hand down my chest to remove it.

"Stop trying to be all macho, Logan. It doesn't suit you. We both know you'll pull a muscle and make me do it."

"Watch me," I shoot back, lifting the tubs with ease and walking past her to the living room. When I get to the doorway, I throw a cocky grin over my shoulder at her, but she doesn't notice. Her hazel eyes flick up and down my back at my exposed skin and straining muscles, her teeth biting into her lower lip.

It seems I'm not the only one struggling to keep my eyes from straying somewhere they shouldn't.

The tubs thud dully against the hardwood floor, causing Felix to glare in my direction.

"What's in these things, anyway?" She wasn't lying when she said they were heavy. Not heavy enough to strain a muscle, but enough that I'm winded from the exertion.

Dani composed herself in the few moments she had as she trailed behind me. She stops at my side, our arms brushing. The elf ears on her head are still tilted sideways, and I reach over and fix them before letting my hand fall down her dark waves.

She doesn't look at me, but her breath stutters before she bends over and clicks the top off the container. "I'm not really sure. The only thing I get out for Christmas is the tree, and I keep that in my closet. I'm sure there's plenty of stuff in here to put up, though." She rummages through the first one before sliding it to the floor and doing the same with the second, pulling out a tangle of Christmas lights.

"Here, I'll start untangling, and you can get the eggnog and music going." I take the giant ball from her, spinning it in my hands to figure out the best way to start.

She crosses the room, calling over her shoulder, "Want whiskey in yours?"

"No shit, Sherlock."

"Fine, then none for you and your ungrateful ass." She tugs open the fridge and pulls out a half gallon of the thick, sweet drink. My mouth waters.

Finding the beginning—or end?—of the ball of lights, I unwind the strands carefully. "Okay, fine. I'm sorry for pointing out the obvious." I add a feminine lilt to my voice before saying, "Yes, Dani, I would love to have whiskey in my eggnog." She mutters something under her breath before there's the scrape of two glasses on the countertop.

Drinks made, Dani places her glass on the coffee table next to our discarded takeout boxes. With a flick of her wrist, Christmas music plays through the speakers. The remote clatters to the table as she walks around it, stopping next to me and holding out my glass. "Here." She doesn't sound angry or annoyed, more somber than anything, as she waits for me to take the glass from her.

"Thank you, Dani," I say with all sincerity. Our fingers brush as I take the glass from her. I'm highly conscious of any type of contact with her, and I think her fingers linger a moment too long before she lets the glass go. "Let's make a toast."

Her face scrunches. "Why?"

"Humor me."

"Fine." She tosses her hands up before picking up her glass and holding it up.

"In memory of Robbie and to traditions both old and new." Dani's hazel eyes widen as they slide up to meet mine. One hand slips to her neck and to the gold chain that hangs there, gripping the charm and sliding it across the chain.

Dani swallows hard, her glass gently tapping against mine. "To Robbie and traditions."

Our eyes are locked as we bring the festive drinks to our mouths and take a sip. I watch as her tongue darts out onto her lip to catch some eggnog, and my dick twitches.

I clear my throat loudly. "Let's get to decorating."

Chapter Four

Danielle

H as Logan always been this good-looking? Shit, I'm staring again. A childhood crush is one thing, but this? Not the same.

He showed up tonight looking like Santa from a wet dream or something. His dark eyes were pleading with me to let him in when I answered the door, and I couldn't leave him out there. Even though I'm mad at him, I still wanted to throw my arms around his neck and hug him tight.

It's what Robbie would've wanted.

The Santa outfit surprised me. It was another thing I thought I'd lost when Robbie died, but Logan meant what he said about the traditions.

He's grown some scruff since the last time I saw him, just enough to make him look more grown up. His light brown hair is still in the same short style that always looked good on him. He's grown out of that lean figure he used to have and has filled out with more muscle, but not enough that he looks cartoonish with giant muscles. He's...manly.

I must be too damn lonely. That's the only plausible explanation for all the fluttering happening right now.

We finished stringing up the lights, put tiny ornaments on my tiny tree, set out a Santa or two, and had a lot—and I mean a lot—of spiked eggnog. Christmas music blares through the speakers as Logan and I dance in my living room.

Somewhere along the way, my hips started moving, and Logan joined in. We're laughing hysterically at our ridiculous and uncoordinated dance moves.

I haven't been this happy in ages.

Felix has long since retreated to a more peaceful spot in the house, so I'm not worried I'll crush the little guy when I flop onto the couch.

Logan's shaking his ass in front of the fireplace, eggnog in hand, and I can't help but giggle. He's a thirty-year-old man, drunk on eggnog and shaking his ass. What's not to laugh at?

My fingers wrap around the gold R of my necklace, squeezing it tight. Robbie feels closer this way, the gold charm keeping him from slipping away from me.

Logan spots me resting on the couch. "Good call. A break sounds good."

I bounce from the force of his flop. "You better not break my couch."

He shoots me a tempting crooked grin. "This fucking thing?" Logan pats the leather. "No way this monster of a couch is breaking."

"If it breaks, you're buying me a new one. An expensive one." The worn leather couch is the same one we dragged here from our parents' house all those years ago.

The laugh he guffaws is fake. "Fine by me."

"Asshole," I say with a chuckle.

Logan's eyes slip closed. I watch enraptured as he sucks in a breath, his shirt pulling tight across his chest.

Tonight's way different from what I thought it would be. Cold, stand-offish, awkward...that's what I was expecting. But it feels so normal. Like it used to be when Robbie was still alive.

Well, except for the way I keep checking him out. I swear, he's made my heart—and other things—pound. Logan's *never* looked this damn good. Or perhaps he was too much like a brother to take notice?

He and Logan were always here. Playing video games, drinking beer, watching football. My life used to be colorful. Fun. But everything faded to gray when Robbie died.

Definitely lonely. Yeah, I'll stick with that. He's familiar and close, and I'm lonely. That's all there is to it.

"Thank you," I whisper as I fiddle with my chain.

"You're welcome," he says automatically, his hand grabbing my knee. "For what?"

"Coming back." There'd come a point a year after Robbie died when I resigned myself to always being alone. Lindsay has been and will always be there for me, but she has her family stuff to worry about, and I don't want to tag along.

Logan seems to sober immediately, his face turning serious. He angles himself to face me, both our heads cradled on the back of the couch. The hand that was resting on my knee reaches up to cup my face, his thumb sliding over my cheek. "I'll always be here, Dani. And I'm sorry it took me so long to come back. I'll regret it for as long as I live."

All the pent-up emotion, the crippling loneliness, and the longing for my brother let loose. Tears slip down my cheeks, my head throbbing with the effort to keep them back. I've been drowning in it for so long, struggling to keep my head above the rolling waves, that the dam bursts.

Logan sits with me as I will the tears to stop falling, for them to dry up and save me the embarrassment of crying in front of him. His thumb brushes away the salty trails, even as they pour down my face.

Everything seems to crash down at once, and it's too much for me to take, so I brush it off. Push it to the side of my mind, barricade it behind a concrete barrier, and focus on something else, anything else, to keep me from completely losing it.

Forced laughter bubbles up my throat, and I push Logan away, wiping my face with a flick of the wrist. "Sorry about that." I turn my back to him to dry my eyes. "Wow, we really made a mess." Discarded

Chinese boxes lay on their sides surrounded by dirty plates and empty eggnog glasses.

I don't dare look back at Logan to see how he's handling my pinballing emotions. Instead, I focus on throwing the trash away and washing the dishes. The task soothes me, settling me into a familiar place.

"Dani, come look at what I found." Logan stands on the other side of the island looking into a tub of Christmas decorations.

I finish rinsing off the last dish and put it on the rack to dry. While I've been busy in the kitchen, Logan's been packing away the Christmas decorations we didn't use.

"Oh, wow. You found a tub. How amazing." I lean against the other side of the counter, cocking my hip.

Logan gives me an exasperated look, clearly fed up with my sarcasm. "Ha, ha. You're hilarious. Look." He unsnaps the lid with a click and tilts the tub in my direction. I'm not quite tall enough, so I rise on my toes to see in. There at the very bottom, covered with glitter snowflake ornaments, are our stockings. We'd searched for them, and I remember checking that tub, but we thought it only had ornaments in it.

"Oh my god." My feet move of their own accord through the kitchen and out into the living room until I'm standing next to Logan. These stockings hold so many memories, not only of Robbie, but of my parents.

Mom made our stockings when we were little, sitting for hours crocheting until she couldn't hold the hook. I wish I would've taken more time to learn when she was still here. I had asked her once when I was ten and got frustrated too easily and quickly gave up.

You always think you have more time before the hourglass runs out.

A comforting hand settles on my shoulder as I pull out our stockings: Mom's, Dad's, Robbie's, Logan's, and mine. We added Logan's the Christmas after my parents died. It's not as personalized as ours. It's a store-bought one, but it belongs right next to ours.

"Did we find the holders somewhere?"

"I think they're over here." Logan's hand drifts down my back before crossing the room to the other tubs. He pops one open and rummages through it. "Got 'em."

I treat each stocking like fine jewels, carrying them as carefully as I can over to where Logan sets the heavy silver stocking holders along the mantle. We hang each stocking and step back, admiring the picturesque view of a blazing fire with stockings and garlands hung decoratively for Christmas.

We're standing so close that I can't help but lean my head against his shoulder, taking support from his quiet strength. I link my hand with his, threading our fingers together.

He's so warm. So comforting. I feel myself relaxing against him, and I sigh.

Logan pulls me close, wrapping me in a tight hug. I fall into it, letting him hold me in a way I haven't been held in a long, long time.

Beneath the thin cover of our clothes, his heart beats in time with mine. I breathe him in, luxuriating in the rich scent of his skin.

Wrapped in his arms, bodies pressed together, my head tucked in the curve of his neck, I'm overwhelmed. I haven't been this close to another person in so long. Felt so much comfort.

My lips press against his neck in a gentle kiss. It's not an innocent peck between friends. No, this kiss lingers.

Logan inhales deeply, his arms gripping me tighter as the atmosphere between us shifts. "Dani."

My heart thumps in my chest. I feel each beat as it pulses in my neck, my fingers...

Maybe it's the whiskey, or the familiarity and sense of home I haven't felt in years when I'm in his arms. But I can't stop myself. I skim my nose up his throat, breathing deeply as my lips press against the corner of his jaw.

My emotions have been building like a tidal wave, and it's all been too much. This feels like the only thing that will help.

Logan is the only thing that can help.

"Dani." His voice is deep and rough. "What are you doing?"

Logan doesn't push me away or tell me to stop. Instead, fingers dig into the flesh of my hips. He swallows hard as I press my lips against the hollow of his throat. "Do you want me to stop?"

Logan groans, tilting his head back. "Dani, we shouldn't."

We as in, he wants this too. Wants me just as badly as I want him.

"Why? There's no one to stop us." I continue kissing his exposed neck, going from one ear to the other, my tongue flicking out against his warm skin.

"You're Robbie's sister." Even as he says the words, he grinds his hips against mine.

My hands slide down his back and hook into the elastic of his Santa pants. "So you don't want me?"

His fingers flex against my hips. I don't give a shit that he's squeezing my love handles. All I care about is the smell of his skin and the heat his touch leaves.

When I press my lips against his skin once more, he groans. "Fuck it." Lips crash against mine, hot and near feral. He tastes of eggnog and whiskey, and I revel in it. Logan kisses me like he's desperate, that he can't wait one more second without his lips touching mine.

I fall into the kiss, drowning in it as it overpowers everything else. All I know now is the tease of his tongue and the taste of his lips.

The headband he forced me to wear is pushed off my head, falling to the floor as his hands stroke through my hair.

"What the fuck are you doing to me?" he growls, his mouth trailing down my neck, nipping and sucking his way down.

I grab his hair, chuckling. "Many things, I hope."

"Not if I get there first." He bends down, his arms sliding under my ass and hauling me up against him. I gasp in shock, clinging onto his shoulders, praying he doesn't drop me.

There's no time for me to process what's happening before my back is against the wall. The heat from the fireplace and Logan's body pressing against me is the most exquisite warmth I've ever felt.

Logan's lips fall onto my neck as I tug up his shirt, loving the feeling of his skin beneath my palms. He groans into my neck, his teeth nipping gently. "Goddamn."

His hips rock against my core, and I gasp. That seems to be the switch that needed flipping because we become a tangle of arms as we both work to get my clothes off.

Free from my shirt, Logan kisses across my chest, his hands kneading my ass as he continues to rock into me, making my head spin. He feels so good pressed against me, but I need more. More than his cock rubbing against me between layers of fabric. I need to feel him, all of him, skin against skin.

"Logan," I plead, my head knocking against the wall. "More."

"More, huh?" He smiles against my skin. "I don't know if you're ready for more, Dani. I think you need more of this." He rocks his hips again, his cock dragging against my clit with unrelenting force.

"Oh, God," I moan, the pleasure toying with me with each thrust of his hips.

The strap of my bra loosens, the confining fabric falling away from my overheated skin.

"You're fucking incredible, Dani. So fucking beautiful." His hot mouth falls on my nipple, sucking as he continues to tease my clit with his cock. All I can do is drown in the pleasure. "Come on, Dani. I know you're close. Come on."

"Logan," I cry as my body surrenders. My orgasm takes me by surprise, ripping through me. I cling to him, my knuckles popping, fisting around the thin fabric of his shirt. Logan's teasing touches, his hot mouth, his breath whispering against my skin, overload my senses.

Body spent, I slump against him. Gentle hands brush my hair out of my face. He's breathless too as he says, "Don't tell me you're too tired now."

"Nope. Not tired." I kiss his neck. "As long as you don't have whiskey dick."

He laughs, the deep rumble of it sending shocks through me. "Not a chance."

The wall leaves my back, and I hold myself tight against him. A strong hand splays across my naked back, the other gripping my ass. Being in his arms gives me a sense of safety, of home, that I've been missing for years.

The cool dark of my room wraps around us like a cloak. He slides me down his body until my feet hit the soft rug, his hands settling on my hips. "I've been wanting you wrapped around my cock all night, and there's nothing that could stop me. Only you."

His eyes dance as he searches my gaze. For a moment, there's no sound except our rushed breaths as we stare at one another. Something passes between us. Recognition. Acceptance. Desire.

We crash together like the waves upon the shore. Logan cups my face, his hot mouth devouring mine. It's a dance of tongues and searching hands. The warm skin of his chest brushes against mine, and my breath hitches. Fingertips dig into my hips before hooking into the elastic of my underwear and dragging them down my thighs. Softness cradles me as Logan presses me into my mattress. Goosebumps follow the trail of his mouth as he kisses me from my neck to below my navel.

His name falls like a prayer from my lips, his breath whispering over my pulsing clit.

"Tell me to stop, Dani, and I will." Logan's gaze travels up my body, locking with mine.

Is this wrong? Should we stop?

Or do I give in to every thought I've had since he got here?

I could linger on how mad I am at him for leaving me, shove him away and live with that anger. Or I could release it. Find comfort in the arms of the only other person who understands.

My fingers drag through his dark hair, my palm resting against his temple. "Don't stop."

I watch as he smiles before placing a kiss on my aching clit.

Logan groans as his tongue slips through my folds. He works magic, teasing, lightly circling my clit just enough to have me gasping and arching into him before slipping away. Still sensitive from my earlier orgasm, it's the most exquisite type of torture.

He's been playing with me, driving me mad. My fingers twist in his hair, and I tug. "Logan, I swear to God—" His rumbling laugh has my pussy clenching.

Then, without warning, Logan thrusts two fingers into my aching pussy. The breath rushes from my lungs at his sudden intrusion. "You getting impatient, Dani? Is this what you wanted?" His fingers thrust into me, his thumb barely grazing my clit.

"Shut up and—oh, fuck." My head digs into the mattress as Logan closes his mouth around my clit and sucks.

He brings me to the edge of another orgasm, only to pull his mouth away. "That's what I thought."

Like it's a game, Logan drags me to the edge, pulling away at the last second. My pussy pulses around his fingers, desperate for a release that won't come.

I'm panting with need, groaning with frustration as he brings me to the brink again. "Logan, please," I beg. "I want to come."

"Do you?" He angles his fingers just right, and I gasp. "How do you want to come, Dani? I could watch your tight pussy squeeze my fingers all night. Taste your sweet cunt and never grow tired." He drags his tongue through my center, more than happy to prove his point. "Tell me what you want, and I'll give it to you. All you have to do is ask."

I grit my teeth, my hips thrusting up for any sort of pressure. All I get is his teasing breath as he chuckles. "Fuck you."

"Say. The. Words." He punctuates each word with the circle of his thumb over my pounding clit.

"Please," I whimper, broken and desperate. "Logan, please let me come."

A satisfied hum fills the space between us before he lowers his head to the apex of my thighs. His fingers move faster, sinking into me at a brutal pace, curling them to hit me just right. Logan suctions his mouth to my clit, and I come undone.

Blinding pleasure rips through me. My body bows off the mattress, my hands tugging on Logan's hair to keep him where I want him as my muscles contract. White spots dance behind my eyes as I lose myself.

Logan doesn't stop, doesn't let up. Even as I trap him between my thighs, his fingers glide through my clenching pussy.

Being with Logan is an out-of-body experience. And now that I've seen a glimpse of what we can be together, I don't want to stop.

Boneless, Logan kisses my inner thigh before settling between my hips. Hot breath cools my overheated skin. I can feel his eyes on me as he hovers above me. "Are you proud of yourself?" I ask, my voice husky.

He lowers his lips to mine, teasing my tongue the same way he teased my pussy. The tip of his cock presses ever so slightly against my opening. "Yeah, I am."

"Don't get too cocky. I'd hate for it to go to your head." My hips rock against him, his tip sinking ever so slowly into me.

He huffs a strangled laugh. "The only thing I'm thinking about right now is how your perfect pussy will feel wrapped around my cock."

Logan pushes into me in one strong stroke. All breath leaves my lungs, my eyes slipping closed at the delicious feeling of fullness. Logan buries his head in my neck as I cling to him.

He pulls back and brushes hair off my cheeks. The soft look in his eyes is one I've never seen before. That look sinks its claws into my heart, and I know it'll never let me go.

Ever so slowly, he moves, never breaking eye contact. It's intimate, more than I thought possible.

"You better not be holding back on me," I tease, as my hips rise to meet his.

Logan lazily rolls his hips, the waves of pleasure building. "What? Not a fan?" He does it again, and I gasp. "C'mon, Dani. Tell me what you want, and you'll have it."

I can't think, can't breathe as he slowly fucks me. My fingers dig into his side, my ankle hooks around his hips, begging him to go deeper. All while never breaking eye contact. "Fuck me, Logan. Own me."

A crooked grin spreads across his face. "There she is."

"Stop toying with me." Nails drag down his back.

I yelp with surprise as Logan sits up and drags me onto his cock. Kneeling between my spread thighs, Logan grips my hips and gives me what I want, driving into me fast and hard. He's dragging his cock along my sensitive front wall, and I'm a whimpering mess, begging him for more.

"Fuck, Dani. Look at you," he says between clenched teeth. "I've been picturing this all night. You spread out like an angel with my cock buried deep inside your pretty little cunt."

My pussy clenches around him, and he groans. He's relentless, pounding into me with powerful thrusts. I'm a mess beneath him, unable to think or breathe. I'm nothing more than his plaything, putty in his hands.

And it's right where I want to be.

I'm almost there, so close to a third orgasm. My cries grow louder, more desperate. "Fuck, fuck, fuck..."

"Eyes on me, Dani. Keep them on me." I do as I'm told, staring into eyes I've known my whole life, but only for the first time, actually *seeing*.

Lust. Desire. A sense of peace. Sadness. It's all there as he circles his thumb around my clit.

I detonate with the most intense orgasm of my life. Unintelligible words fall from my mouth as white spots dance in my vision, blocking my view of Logan.

With a curse, Logan pulls out, stroking his cock once, twice, and then spilling his release on my stomach.

I'm too dazed and sexed-out to worry about the mess. I'm floating in orgasmic bliss.

Logan's panting, dropping onto the mattress beside me, arm tossed over his face. I stare at his muscled back when he sits up. Red scratches bloom across his back. He sighs, running a hand down his face before he stands. "I'll get you a washcloth."

My eyes settle on the ceiling as I listen to his retreating footsteps. It doesn't take long for my overheated skin to cool. Even less time for reality to set in.

I just had sex with my brother's best friend.

34

Chapter Five

Danielle

Logan's in the bathroom. Water runs. Cabinets clatter closed.

Without him here, his body pressed next to mine, an overwhelming sense of panic whooshes over me.

What have we done?

Unable to move thanks to Logan, in more ways than one, I cover my face with my hands.

Shit. Shit. Shit.

What have I done?

This wasn't a good idea. I mean, *Logan*? I had sex with Logan. And the worst part? I *liked* it. More than liked. I loved it.

Fingers dig into my eyeballs as if to scrape away the memory of his cocky smile between my thighs. "Oh my God," I groan.

"Am I interrupting your freak-out?"

I freeze.

No. No. No. No.

I look at him through my parted fingers. Logan leans against the door frame, wearing boxers and holding a dripping washcloth. He jabs a thumb over his shoulder. "I can leave and come back when you're done."

Despite my freak-out, I laugh. "Well, I can't do it now, can I? I've been caught red-handed."

He walks around the bed before sitting beside me. "Will it make you feel better to know I did the same thing?"

I shrug. "Maybe."

"You mind if I..." he holds up the washcloth.

He was inside me ten minutes ago, but the feeling in the room has shifted. It's tense. Awkward. I fight the growing urge to cover myself, and nod.

With sure fingers, Logan cleans me up. He touches me only with the washcloth, and though it's strange, I wish that his skin would brush against mine.

It's all so confusing.

Finally clean, I take a quick shower. When I return to my bedroom, Logan's there, muscles tight. Dark eyes watch me as I crawl into bed.

"The least you could do is cuddle with me." I wave him over, patting the bed next to me.

He pulls back the covers. "I didn't know if you're the cuddling type."

I snort. "Well, we're learning a lot about each other tonight."

Logan lifts his arm, and I snuggle into him, resting my head on his chest. I trace his chest with a finger, listening to his heartbeat, lulled by the rise and fall of his chest.

It's dark in my room. Through the window, the street light illuminates the flurries of falling snow. It's quiet. Peaceful.

Soft lips press against my temple. "Merry Christmas, Dani." Logan's arms wrap around me, holding me tight.

Despite what's happened in the past three years, despite the fact that my head is all mixed up about what just happened, there's no other place I'd rather be.

"Merry Christmas."

Felix jumps onto the bed with a quiet meow. My head bobbles as Logan jumps. "That fucking cat."

"Hey," I say, snatching up the gray fur ball and tucking him under my chin. "He's a good boy, aren't you, Felix?"

"I don't think he likes me very much."

"You're just new," I say, leaning back against his chest. "You're a stranger." I kiss Felix's head. "We don't like strangers, do we?"

Felix leaps from my arms, hopping off the bed and slipping into the darkness.

"He doesn't like you either," Logan laughs.

"Oh, shut up. We have an understanding." Meaning, I love him; he tolerates me. Most days.

"Sure," he scoffs.

"At least he's not like Roxie. She would've bitten your face off by now." Our childhood dog was the most devilish dachshund I've ever met. Every time Logan came over, all she did was follow him around and growl, nipping at his ankles when he wasn't paying attention.

Logan groans, a hand lifting to swipe down his face. "That dog was the devil incarnate. Do you remember when Robbie left his bedroom door open while I was sleeping on the floor and she bit my nose?"

I remember it well.

Laughter bubbles up my throat. "That wasn't Robbie," I manage between heaving laughs. "That was me."

"What?"

"I let Roxie in."

Logan sits up, jostling me. "You're the reason she bit the shit out of my nose? I have a scar." He points to the barely there scrape down the bridge of his nose, his mouth curling with held-back laughter.

"Let me see." I hold his chin, tilting his head left and right in the dim lighting. "It adds character. I'm sure you tell all the ladies it's from a fight."

He shakes his head, moving over me to pin me to the mattress. "The only *lady* I want is the one who apparently gave me the scar."

A rush pulses through me at his closeness. "I hate to break it to you, but Roxie died a long time ago."

Logan's eyes flicker to my mouth. All I want is to feel his lips against mine. "Fuck Roxie."

Then with a fierceness I crave, Logan kisses me. I forget how to speak, how to think, how to breathe. All I know is the taste of him. The tease of his tongue. His weight pressing against me. When he pulls away, I'm breathless, near delirious.

"Fuck, I'll never get used to that." His voice is deep, rough with need, and I shiver. My eyes slide open, his face inches away. His eyes shutter closed, and he sighs as if pained to say his next words. "Are we going to talk about this?"

I trail my hands over his shoulders to grip his neck. Sheets ruffle as I nod.

With a deep sigh, Logan plops next to me. I study his profile, nerves fluttering. I don't have to think about what I want because I already know.

Logan rolls to face me. "Dani, all I know is that I've wanted you since I stepped through that door tonight. Being with you, feeling you—I haven't felt anything like it. And kissing you just now? I don't want to look at you and not be able to taste your lips again."

Oh shit.

My heart pounds in my chest, and I suck in a breath. "Same."

Logan laughs through an exhale. "Really, Dani?"

"What? Do you want me to give a long, drawn-out explanation, or for me to get straight to the point?"

"I don't know. Maybe a guy wants to hear that the woman he made come three times wants to do it again."

I gasp in shock. "You were *counting*?"

"Of course I was," he says nonchalantly. "And the sounds you made—"

"Okay. That's enough."

He laughs, pulling me onto his chest. "Relax. It's late, and I have an early morning."

"Family Christmas?"

"Yeah." Fingers absentmindedly make patterns down my arm. "I haven't been since, well, you know."

I nod against his chest, settling into his warmth, falling asleep to the sound of his heart and the soothing comfort of his touch.

What feels like minutes later, I'm woken up by a very handsome, very sleep-rumpled Santa. "Sorry, I didn't mean to wake you." The oversized red fluffy coat hangs open as Logan kisses my forehead.

I groan. "What time is it?"

"Early." He brushes hair off my forehead. "I've got to head back to the hotel and change."

A tired chuckle bubbles from my lips. "I'm sure your nieces and nephew would love it."

His grin is addicting. "I'm sure they would." Logan inhales deeply before pressing his lips to mine in a warm kiss. "Go back to sleep."

"I don't know. Watching you make the walk of shame dressed as Santa seems pretty appealing right now."

"No shame here, baby," he says with a laugh. "Can I come back later?"

"Hmmhmm."

"Good." He leans in to kiss me one more time, but I don't want him to go. The kiss grows deeper, and Logan groans as he pulls away. "See you later."

Chapter Six

Logan

The house is far too loud this morning. There's a slight ache between my eyes thanks to the whiskey from last night. But it's also Christmas morning, and those are always loud.

My nieces and nephew run loops through the house. Christmas was exciting growing up, but I don't remember it being *this* exciting. One by one, they dart through the room, screeching like pterodactyls.

Definitely not helping in the headache department.

My eyes pinch closed, and I stroke a hand down my face. What the fuck did I get myself into last night?

I don't regret it, not for one second. But shit, what would Robbie think?

He'd kill me for sleeping with his little sister.

I exhale heavily. I can't blame the alcohol for what happened with Dani—I wanted her before a drop passed my lips—but I can blame it for the way I'm feeling right now.

The couch dips next to me. "I'm amazed you're here. Thought it'd be another Logan-less year. But I guess the world would explode if we were all here at the same time. Good thing Miles has that covered. Saved us from extinction." Brittney folds her feet underneath her, a steaming mug of coffee in her hands.

I snort a laugh. "Where is our mysterious brother?" I ask, eyes darting around the chaos of the living room. The kids tore through the wrappings, and no one bothered to tell them to clean up their mess.

Thick, decorative paper and sparkly tissue cover the carpet, frequently getting kicked by my nieces and nephew as they dart around.

Of my two younger brothers, Miles is the wild child of the family. I was always gone with Robbie, and he was always with Gramps. They had a relationship that I was sometimes jealous of, but he needed someone like I needed Robbie. Can't fault him for that.

Cooper, my youngest brother, is the most responsible of the six of us. He's working in the ER and won't be here until this afternoon to enjoy our Christmas meal. He takes up these holiday shifts so his co-workers can spend the morning with their families.

"Cabin." Brittney blows over the top of her mug, humming with content as she takes a sip.

I nod and lean back against the couch. I'm not surprised he's hiding away out there. But I guess there's no room for me to judge, because I've done the same damn thing for three years.

"Aww, you two look cute. Whoa." My youngest sister, Allison, is nearly taken out at the knees as the kids swerve around her.

Brittney does what any mom would, yelling at her three-year-old. "Arianna, slow down."

She doesn't, of course.

More screaming makes me wince.

"Henry, Lucy, do I have to tell you again?" My oldest sister Carly barks out from the kitchen, where she helps Mom with the food.

They slow just enough to avoid getting in trouble.

Allison sits on my other side, her small hand slapping against my arm. "Move over."

Dani's bed is looking real good right now. I'd rather have her crowding my space than my sisters.

The thought of "crowding" her space again brings a secret smile to my face.

Allison nudges me with a shoulder. "I saw that smile."

"I don't know what you're talking about. I had an itch."

Allison scoffs. "Uh-huh, sure." She wraps a blanket around her shoulders as if she's trying to cocoon herself in the soft fabric. "How'd it go last night? Dani doing okay?"

Why do I tell my sister anything? Of all my siblings, Allison's the one I talk to the most. Maybe it's because she's my baby sister, or it could be because she's vicious when it comes to gathering information, and keeping a secret from her is nearly impossible. She's persistent as shit too, so dodging her calls isn't worth it.

Brittney gasps, and I close my eyes desperately trying to make this conversation disappear. "Oh, Dani. How's she doing? God, I can't imagine what she's going through. How hard it must be, especially during the holidays."

I clear my throat to prepare for the onslaught I'm about to get. "She's doing as well as you think she would."

After last night, I'd say we're both doing better.

Three times better.

"What's she doing today? You should go get her," Allison chimes.

"Yes! Go get her." Brittney sits up, almost spilling her coffee.

I shake my head. "I don't think—"

"Who are we getting?" Mom sticks her head around the corner, a kitchen towel dangling from her hand.

Fuck me. "No one."

"Dani," Brittney says at the same time. "We think he should go pick her up and bring her over here."

Mom's blue eyes soften. "Oh, I would love that. I think that's wonderful." Carly stands next to Mom as she talks, her apron spotted with some sort of food splatter, and asks Mom what we're talking about.

I toss my arms wide, head whipping back and forth. "For the love of God, where's Dad? Or Chris?" I'm completely overpowered by the women in my life and need someone to back me up, whether it's my dad or my brother-in-law.

Carly dismisses my questions with a wave of her hand. "Something about Christmas lights."

A little body slams against the back of her legs, bouncing off her before tumbling to the floor. My oldest sister grabs her son's arm, chastising him as Lucy and Ari continue running.

"Go get her," Allison says again, smacking my arm.

Arguing with them is pointless. With no one to back me up, I'm at their mercy. They don't know Dani like I do, and I don't think she'd enjoy being here. But with my three sisters and mother pressuring me, I break.

"Fine," I sigh in exasperation. "I'll call and see if she wants to come." I reach for my phone on the coffee table, but Brittney snags it before I do.

"No, go get her. You can't give her a choice in this. Plus, you're more convincing in person."

"You want me to take her against her will?" I ask mockingly.

"We're not telling you to kidnap her." Allison rolls her eyes. "Dani's stubborn, like someone else I know. You just need to give her a little push. Now get going." Allison nudges my shoulder.

Even as they shove me out the door, I can't help but hope Dani says yes.

COLD WIND WHIPS THROUGH the streets, snow swirling in its wake as I push the buzzer to Dani's apartment. It stopped snowing during the night, leaving two inches on the ground. Nothing like last year's avalanche that Carly brings up any chance she gets.

"Yeah?" Dani's voice has an electronic tinge through the speaker.

"It's me."

"Hmmm... I don't think I know anyone by that name. You must have the wrong building."

"Smartass. Let me in, please? It's freezing out here." My breath billows in front of me, and I bounce on my feet to ward off the cold.

Her laugh rings through the speaker. "Fine. Only because you asked nicely."

Dani waits for me at the top of the stairs, her arms crossed as she leans against the door frame. My eyes trail up her legs and linger on her hips before snagging on her bright red Christmas cat sweater. "What's that?"

Dani looks down at the sad cat wearing a Santa hat and tinsel scarf. Little lights flicker festively across her torso. "Don't hate on my Christmas Cat. He and Felix are my Christmas companions." She steps back, letting me into her apartment. "I thought you weren't coming back 'til later."

"I've been sent on a mission."

A fire blazes in the fireplace, its warmth reaching the door. Some Christmas movie plays on the TV, most likely one of those cheesy ones Brittney and Carly forced me to watch as a kid. Felix lies curled in a ball on the couch, not giving two shits about me.

Without meaning to, my eyes linger on Robbie's door.

"Really?" she sing-songs, taking her place on the couch next to Felix. Her eyes narrow. "Okay, I'll bite. What's this mission you speak of?"

"First," I hold up a finger. "I want you to know that I was forced into this."

Dani blows a raspberry. "What every girl wants to hear."

"Two," my middle finger joins my first. "I hope that you'll say yes." The wood floor creaks beneath my feet as I move to sit on the coffee table in front of her. "My family is inviting you to spend the afternoon with us. Before you say no," I cut her off before a sound comes from her parted lips. "It's just for food and company, and I know there's nothing to eat here."

Her hazel eyes fall to the floor in contemplation, her voice soft as she says, "I'm not sure."

I reach out, cupping her knee. The simple touch burns my hand, makes it itch with the need to slide up her thigh. To make her moan.

45

Not the time, I remind myself. Later.

I can see the hesitation on her face, so I play the one card I have left. "Robbie wouldn't want you to be alone."

Dani's eyes shoot to my face. "That's a low blow."

I shrug. "Maybe. But it's true."

Felix grumbles as Dani scoops him into her arms. She strokes down his back, his grumbling transforming into purrs. "I don't know if I'll be able to handle it."

The vulnerability in her statement has me moving to the couch, wrapping my arms around her, and holding her close. Dani settles against me, exhaling.

"After Robbie...Christmas is hard for me, too." Felix seems to purr more loudly. I can feel his gentle rumble against Dani's body. "It's not as hard now. Not when you're with me."

Every word is true. I've avoided anything that made me think of my best friend. I ran away from everything: my family, Dani, myself...but now that I'm here, facing the things I left behind, *who* I left behind, it's different.

She swallows. "Can we come back here after?" Pleading, tear-filled eyes meet mine.

"We'll come right back." Light and hope fill my chest. Tentatively, I close the space between us and place my lips on hers in a soft kiss.

Dani pulls back, with a hint of a smile on her face. "I'll need an exit signal."

"What, like pulling your ear?" I brush her hair back, tucking it behind her ear.

"Would putting on my shoes and walking out the door be too subtle?"

I bark a laugh. "As long as you don't wear that god-awful sweater."

Dani swats me in the chest. Felix makes a grand escape, thumping to the floor and darting away. "I might wear this to spite you." She pushes off the couch, leaving me to stare after her. Dani turns when she reaches the bathroom. "You won't leave me alone, will you?"

The look in her eyes, the arch of her brow, the worry in her voice. She's not talking about lunch with my family.

It's deeper than that.

All it takes is three steps for me to cross the room. I cup her face, lifting her gaze to mine, and pray she sees the truth in my eyes. "I'm done leaving."

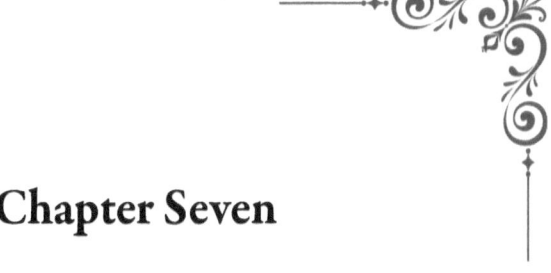

Chapter Seven

Danielle

Spending the day with Logan's family was actually *nice*. There's no hollow feeling in my chest, or an ache in my heart that won't fade. I feel...light.

Having Logan back, if only for a short time, has somehow changed everything. I was hesitant about going with him—about this whole thing, really—but it's exactly what I needed.

What we both needed.

It seems impossible, but I forgot how large the Miller family is, and they've only expanded through the years. They all welcomed me with open arms. Literally. I was greeted with warm hugs that made me feel right at home.

The Miller family was close with ours growing up. Our houses were on the same block, so summer days were spent running around with the neighborhood kids. Robbie and I kept to our friends. He and Logan were running around while Lindsay and I played with dolls.

When Mom and Dad died in a car accident, Mrs. Miller constantly invited Robbie and me for dinner, even going as far as dropping meals off after my aunt went back to her life.

Aunt Chasity tried her best. She wanted to take me in, but Robbie wasn't having it. He was already eighteen and didn't want me hours away. So he stepped up and took care of me. Aunt Chasity checks in from time to time, but we're not close.

Not like Logan's family.

They all have the same look to them; the same shade of brown hair and eyes, a similar dimple on one cheek.

His sisters are exactly how I remember them being. Carly's all poise, Brittney's warm, while Allison's boisterous and teasing, just like her oldest brother.

The brothers, though, couldn't be more different. Cooper has always been quiet and polite, more comfortable watching the chaos than being in it, silently laughing at the conversation. I was most curious about the bad-boy brother, Miles. There might be something brewing between Logan and me, but Miles was Lindsay and I's biggest crush. The hair, those eyes, the attitude...I'm pretty sure every girl in a ten-mile radius had a crush on him. I'm disappointed that he was a no-show.

Listening to the siblings bicker at the dinner table was both a blessing and a curse. It served as a harsh reminder of what I had and lost. It dragged memories to the surface. Pleasant ones that don't sting of a past life. Ones where we laugh and tease.

Logan must've seen me struggling to hold my composure as we ate. His warm hand slipped into mine under the table, away from the eyes of his family.

His touch comforts me. Last night might've been out of character for both of us, but it's also *right*. Three years ago, I would never have dreamed of Logan holding my hand, touching my skin, kissing my lips. But now that he has, I don't think I can live without it.

For too long, I've been alone. Alone with the loss, the heartbreak. But having him here, knowing he's feeling the same searing pain in his chest since Robbie died, in a fucked up way, it's comforting.

But that pain? It's less when he's near. Logan's encouragement helps me breathe easier. I wonder if it's the same for him.

We don't stay long. No need for a super-secret escape signal, not that we solidified one. Going from being all alone to being surrounded by a warm family left me wide-eyed and dazed.

Glancing at Logan, it seems he's feeling as worn down as I am. We're back at my apartment building, his eyes downcast as we walk up the steps.

Not too tired, though, because his hands rest on my hips while I work to unlock the door. Logan brushes my hair away from my neck, planting soft kisses there. His breath tickles against my skin, leaving goosebumps in its wake. "If you keep doing that, we'll never get inside."

He hums against my skin. "Don't care." A bone-deep shiver echoes through me. He's wrapped around me like a warm blanket, one that I don't want to move from.

"You'll care when old lady Humphry next door comes out and starts whacking you with her cane. She's a dangerous one." The lock clicks open, my keys jangling as I pull them free.

Logan pauses, his head lifting off my shoulder. "Seriously?" I can picture him tilting his head like a puppy in disbelief.

"No," I laugh, pushing the door open. "But I wouldn't put it past her." Mrs. Humphry's a spunky old lady, but she's nice enough to me. She walks with a cane, and though I've seen her use it to swat people's ankles, I doubt she'd come out here now.

Keys clatter into the bowl on the entry table. I'm too busy pulling cold, wet boots off my feet to pay attention to Logan. They plop onto their sides, and I bend over, placing them on the shoe rack.

It's quiet. Too quiet. No rustling of a winter coat or the thud of a shutting door. Curious, I glance back and roll my eyes. I should've known better.

Logan stands frozen in the doorway, hands braced on either side of the frame, hungry eyes glued to my ass. The look he's giving is unholy.

My throat goes dry. "What?" I ask playfully. "See something you like?"

Wood groans beneath his clenched fists. "I might go to hell for it, but yeah," he sighs, finally stepping into the apartment. "I do."

His expression flickers with indecision. His eyes burn, yet there's something more there. Reluctance, maybe? Those lips thin into a firm line. Logan sucks in a breath through his nose, his eyes shuttering closed.

It's easy to know what he's thinking. The same thing has been playing in my head on repeat. He's my dead brother's best friend. We shouldn't be happening, but we are.

I clasp his face between my hands and kiss him gently. "Then I'll be right there with you."

Robbie's never far from my mind. I understand his sense of guilt, because I feel it too.

What would Robbie think of all this? Would he be okay with the two of us together?

My gut tells me he'd want us to be happy. If that means us being together, then he'd approve. Probably not before he whooped Logan's ass, but still.

A hint of a smile pulls at his lips. He rests his forehead against mine. Then, ever so slowly, Logan lowers his mouth to mine. The kiss is tender, meant to seek comfort, but it doesn't take long for it to grow and transform into desperate need.

Logan slips his arms around me, his hand fisting my hair at the base of my neck, guiding my lips where he wants them. I open to him, moaning around his tongue.

It's a need so desperate that it grows more urgent no matter how often we sate it.

My hip bumps against the entryway table, rattling the objects on top of it. Logan presses into me, and I can feel the hard length of him against my stomach.

Being with Logan is as easy as breathing. He stokes a flame with the brush of his hand. Breaks through my defenses with a swipe of his tongue. Sends my heart pounding with a simple glance.

It doesn't take long for us to fall into ravenous hunger. I can't seem to get enough of him. We're a storm of frenzied touches, clawing at our clothing until we're skin against skin.

Furniture clatters, wood scrapes, knick-knacks jostle. The apartment could crumble around us, and I wouldn't care so long as he's touching me. His every touch is a balm to my senses, working both to end my misery and stoke my burning desire.

Logan lowers us to the floor, tugging off what little clothing is left. The cold of the floor seeps into my back, and I shiver. His eyes flare with recognition, and he reaches for the coffee table, igniting the fireplace with the click of a button. Heat washes over me, both from the flames and from his gaze.

I'm on display for him, and yet I don't cower from it. He's made it clear he loves my body, so I flaunt it for him. Only him. I run my hands down my breasts and across my nipples. Logan's eyes blaze hotter than the fire, his teeth sinking into his bottom lip as he hurriedly fumbles for his pants to grab a condom.

"Logan," I pant, my hand sliding lower down my body. I'm wet for him and pulsing with intense need. The package of the condom rips as my fingers graze over my clit.

"That's mine," he growls, swiping my hand away before pinning my arms over my head.

"Is it?" I tease, pressing my body against his. "Last I checked, it's mine."

Logan nips at my lips. "Your body is mine to play with. Mine to enjoy." With a fierceness so breathtaking, Logan devours my mouth. I melt against him. Gone is the teasing, because he was right. I'm putty in his hands.

When he breaks our kiss, I'm a panting mess. Lips trail down neck, tongue flicking over my sensitive nipples before planting sweet kisses on my soft belly. Rough hands glide over my thighs, pushing them open. "Mine."

The wet heat of his mouth engulfs me. He groans with pleasure against my pussy, making me gasp. I'm lost to the sensation, my hips bucking desperately against him. My entire body is shaking with anticipation and pleasure, my breasts bouncing with each heaving breath. I reach for him, fingers grasping for anything to hold on to, anything to keep me grounded in this moment.

Like a spring drawn tight, I'm ready to explode from the exploration of his tongue. Logan's grip around my thighs tightens as he pushes them farther apart until I'm fully open to him. He drags his tongue lazily across my folds. "You're mine, Dani. Say it."

"Yours."

"That's right," he growls, sitting up to kneel between my spread legs. A smug smile pulls at his sinful mouth.

I've never needed anyone more. Not just right now, with me aching and ready, watching as he hits his cock at my center. No, I need him here, in my life, and that thought hits deep.

The squeeze of his hands on my hips pulls me back to this moment.

Slowly, so slowly, he presses into me. We both groan as he seats himself deep, my eyes shuttering closed as I give in to the pleasure.

Logan plants soft kisses on my cheeks and my forehead, so tender that tears gather.

I press a palm to his rough cheek, holding on to this moment.

Unlike last night, he takes things slower. Each thrust is smooth and lazy as if he's taking his time, memorizing this moment.

The reflection of the flames dancing in his eyes is mesmerizing, but it's not what's setting me on fire. He is.

"Logan, faster," I beg, needing to chase the heat he's set in me.

His lips pull up in a cocky grin. "Say please." He keeps his strokes steady and drives me wild.

"Pretty please, Logan. Fuck me." I'm whining from need, but I don't care. I need him to lose control. My hands grip his ass, begging him to move faster.

"Since you asked so nicely," he grits out through clenched teeth, swallowing a moan as he picks up his pace. Logan reaches for my knee, hitching it higher to rest on his side, changing the angle of his movement.

"Yes," I hiss, my hips rocking with his. My orgasm is close, boiling just beneath the surface. Fire spreads across my skin, sweat beading on both our brows as we chase our pleasure. He thrusts deep, his hips moving at a relentless pace. With a cry, my body writhes against his, my pussy fluttering around him as my orgasm takes hold, stealing my breath and making me see stars.

"Dani," my name sounds like a prayer. Logan's face drops to my neck, his movements growing frantic. "Dani." Teeth pinch my soft flesh, muffling his moans as he finds his release.

I hold him close to me as we catch our breaths. He said he wouldn't leave, and I close my eyes, hoping he holds on to that promise. Because if he doesn't, I don't know if I'll be able to pick up the pieces.

Chapter Eight

Logan

Dani's sound asleep. Her deep, even breaths do nothing to comfort the raging storm within me.

I'm restless. There's a buzzing just beneath my skin: a raging hornets' nest, furious and unrelenting.

It shouldn't be like this. I spent the rest of the day tangled up in Dani, surrounded by her warmth. So why am I feeling like this?

Careful not to disturb her, I slip from the sheets, closing her bedroom door with a muted thud. Something's been nagging at me, and I think I've finally found the strength to face it.

Coming home. Being back here. Facing everything I've run away from for the past three years...

Almost everything.

There's still one thing I need to do.

The Christmas tree flickering in the corner is the only light in the apartment. A flick of a tail in the corner of my eye announces my companion. Perched on the island, Felix watches me with narrowed eyes, tail furling. I hold my hands up in caution. That gray fluff ball might have Dani wrapped around his claws, but I see him for the patient predator he is. Under his haunting gaze, I cross the room, a weight bracing on my shoulders.

Like a dark void, the solid wood of Robbie's bedroom door taunts me. All the memories and reminders of him and his life shut tight behind it. Dani told me she doesn't go in there, and I understand that. She's been facing grief, living day-to-day, feeling the weight of her loss while I ran.

Dani's shown me that leaning on each other, taking the strength the other offers, and going through it together, facing it head-on, is better than denying it.

Cold wood grain presses against my palm. I breathe deeply, working to settle the storm of emotion unsettling every anchor I've placed. Reminders of Robbie, of our friendship, are right behind this door.

Only if I have the strength to open it.

The wood turns warm under my touch as I stand rooted in place. My fingers ache where they're clenched around the doorknob, ready for when I gain enough courage to face what I left behind. But I can't bring myself to do it. The urge to turn around, to slide back into bed with Dani is strong. But what good would that do me? I'd go back to living a half-life, numb and exhausting, running from family—from her.

My legs tingle, my feet turning to ice the longer I stand here, working through the full force of the grief of losing my best friend. His voice echoes in the back of my mind, mocking me. *"Just do it, asshole."*

Tears fall as I shut my eyes. Soothing cool air fills my lungs. I exhale slowly and twist the knob. The mechanism clicks, and I pause. All I have to do is push it open and face what I ran from all those years ago. With a gentle creak, the door sways open.

Stale air hits my face. Robbie's room is frozen in time. Yellow light from the streetlights filters in through the partially open blinds, the curtains on either side like sentries keeping watch. The bed is made in the traditional Robbie way; the comforter is thrown over the sheets so that it looks made, but isn't. Loose change speckles the wooden top of the dresser, but it's the pictures that catch my eye.

Old family photos, the only kind they'll have, with all four of them smiling at the camera. A fishing trip with his dad, getting a kiss on the cheek from his mom, toddler Robbie holding a furious-looking infant Dani. Each one makes me smile at the memory of the life he had.

There's one picture partially hidden behind the rest. The polished corner of a wooden frame peeks out from the back, cleaner than the others. A coating of dust rests on every surface except this one.

A cautious breath releases as I lift the frame, my thumb wiping away what little dust rests on the glass.

My palms sweat; my steady hand trembles. I stumble backward until my ass hits the mattress, eyes locked on the picture within the frame. A photo I've never seen before stares back at me. The two of us hold up half-empty drinks, our eyes glassy. Robbie's laughing, his head tossed back as his beer sloshes close to the rim. I'm red-faced with laughter, almost doubled over.

I don't remember taking this picture, but it opens the dam that I've been holding back for far too long.

All sense of time disappears as the devastating grief washes over me in suffocating waves. Muffled tears turn into heaving sobs.

The picture blurs, morphing into a prism of colors, until it fades entirely. Each shuddering breath is harsher than the last. I'm raw nerves, exposed and bleeding. Nothing can ease the downpour or numb the sorrow.

I forget to be quiet, forget to dampen my cries as I let it all out. The outside world fades away, the tunnel leading me back sealing off as I mourn.

Anger, hurt, sorrow, regret, guilt. Each emotion rolls through me without end.

He's gone.

My best friend is gone.

What were the last words I said to him? The last time I saw him, laughing and smiling like he was in that picture?

He was supposed to have his whole life ahead of him. He was always supposed to be here.

Never again will we spend Saturdays watching college football. No more late nights downtown.

My best friend is gone.

I'm so lost to the world around me I don't notice the creak of the door, or the small hands that run through my hair. Soothing words I don't hear fall in a hush around me. I cling to the soft shape before me, burying my face into the only thing comforting me.

Once the fog clears and my tears have dried do I realize Dani's with me. I'm wrapped around her, lying on Robbie's bed, her soothing hand gliding down my back. We're both sniffling, her chest rising and falling with soft hiccups. The room is still, quiet in the relative darkness. Neither of us speaks, still battling with emotions or sitting in the stillness with them. They'll always be there. This ever-present part of ourselves, but acknowledging them, and living with them is far better than suppressing them.

"I'm sorry," I whisper in a voice hoarse from crying. "I didn't mean to—"

"Hush." She slides her fingers into my hair, the other stroking my back. "You don't have anything to apologize for." Soft lips press against my forehead, and I shut my eyes at the tenderness there. "It was time, Logan."

I nod, burrowing into her softness. Something hard presses into my elbow. I reach for it, fingers scraping across wood and glass as I grab the picture frame. The picture that brought everything to the surface stares back at me. "Where did this come from?"

Dani sits up, and I shift my weight, letting her rest against the headboard before I cling to her once more. "I brought it in here," she says, taking it from me.

My eyebrows furrow. "I thought you said you never come in here?"

"Only once," she starts, her fingers softly brushing more dust away. "Do you remember this night?" I shake my head and rub my thumb against her soft thigh. "I had just turned twenty-one. You and Robbie dragged me out to buy me drinks, but the two of you ended up getting drunk. He insisted on taking a picture." She laughs at the memory. "Said

I needed to document the moment when I was finally drinking legally. The three of us took one, but it was blurry. You were making fun of me, being a pain like you always are, and made Robbie laugh. I took the picture." She sucks in a shaky breath. "You deserved to be next to the pictures on his dresser. You were our family. Are our family. It's the only time I walked past that door until tonight when I heard you."

Sitting up, I cup her jaw and wipe away her silent tears. "I never should've left. I'm sorry for that."

Dani shakes her beautiful head, smiling softly at me. "You're here now. That's what matters."

I kiss her softly, tenderly expressing my regret and my promises. Because I'm not going anywhere now that I've found her again. She's the light that streaks across a black sky, and I'm not going back to the darkness.

Chapter Nine

Danielle

Having Logan back feels like a fever dream. The time between Christmas and New Year's Eve settles into a pattern that I'm more than happy to be in. Logan spends each night tangled around me, kissing me before sending me out the door to work.

It's strange—feeling at peace again.

But I can't help but feel like the other shoe is about to drop. That this time with Logan is a blip. It will soon disappear as if it never happened. That life will return to what it's been for the past three years.

The humming dread grows steadier with each passing day.

Arms wrap around my waist. Warm lips press against my neck. "I'm heading out." Logan's gaze meets mine in the mirror. "You look beautiful."

I laugh. "I haven't done anything yet." My face is pink from the warm water I washed it with. Dark hair slips free from the quick bun, held back by the reindeer headband I found tossed on the floor.

"Even better."

"You're so full of shit." Even as I say the words, I can't help but lean into him.

His deep chuckle sends shivers down my spine. Logan kisses my neck once more. "Maybe. But not about this."

My mouth pops open, but I'm silenced by the buzz of a ringing phone.

Logan doesn't even look at the screen before saying, "I'll be right down."

I turn in his arms, leaning back against the bathroom counter. "Gotta run?"

He nods. "Cooper's parked outside."

Logan and his youngest brother have been hatching a plan to sneak attack their brother, Miles. I won't tell Logan, but I always had a crush on his bad-boy little brother. Apparently, he's reformed now, living in their grandpa's cabin tucked away in the woods.

"Time to go shake the hornet's nest?"

Strong hands squeeze my hips. "Oh, yeah. Don't be surprised if I come back bruised."

A smile tugs at my lips. "You'd probably deserve it."

With a snort, Logan kisses me. "Probably." He gives me one last lingering kiss before pulling away. "Have fun with Lindsay. I'll be back tomorrow."

He tosses a wave over his shoulder before I lock the door behind him.

Felix twitches his tail from his perch on the couch. He's still not a fan of Logan, but he's coming around. Ironic, considering we might not see him again.

We haven't talked about what happens when he leaves. I want to believe him when he says he's not running off again, but there's that niggling part in the back of my mind that constantly reminds me that he's done it once, he'll do it again.

FELIX WINDS THROUGH my legs, meowing for attention. I left him alone for one night, and here he is, acting like he was utterly abandoned.

I can relate.

Pretty sure that's how I'll be feeling all over again when Logan leaves. Which I definitely shouldn't be thinking about or I'll start crying.

"Look at us." Felix purrs against my chest, his head bumping my shoulder. "Two peas in a pod."

I always knew he would leave, but it was in the distant future. Now though, I can't deny the churning sense of dread in my gut.

How I went from hating him, never wanting to see his stupid face again, to dreading him leaving and never coming back seems insane.

Nine days.

That's all it took for Logan to weasel his way back into my life, and my heart. Against my better judgement, I opened the door to him, one that I thought was sealed shut, and let him flop onto my couch and dig his claws in.

The apartment feels empty without him. Logan's presence is like throwing a pebble into a lake; it reverberates into every corner. Without him in it, it's like a coffin.

When did my apartment go from home to...this?

Felix wiggles out of my arms, feet thumping on the floor as he prances to the couch.

My eyes are heavy and puffy from lack of sleep. I slept in Lindsay's bed, but she's no replacement for Logan. Her hitching breaths were nothing like his soft snores.

I clasp my necklace, the gold letters clinking. For all her fretting, Lindsay's an amazing gift giver. First with Felix and now with my parents' initials hanging next to Robbie's. Now, all three are close to my heart.

Did Logan struggle to sleep like I did? Is he missing me as much as I'm missing him? Will he feel the hollowness that's already spreading through my chest?

The charms zip along the chain, but it doesn't help the growing anxiety currently churning in my chest.

Sleep. It'll cure all ailments of the Logan variety.

I sigh when my head hits the pillow. Even my sheets smell like him, which is both comforting in ways I didn't know existed until now, and infuriating. But now that I'm home, in the space we've shared, I can't sleep.

All I can think of is him.

For hours I lay in bed, tossing and turning, replaying what it was like three years ago, losing the two most important people in my life in one fell swoop.

Again.

It's a pain I've long since gotten used to, but now? The sting is sharper than it's ever been. Because it's happening all over again, and there's nothing I can do to stop it. Especially now that things between Logan and me are different.

He's not my brother's annoying, if cute, best friend. He's a man who feels like home. The only person I'd let close enough to break down my barrier and wiggle his way back into my life.

And he's leaving.

Tears drip down my cheeks, soaking into the pillowcase.

This is ridiculous. I shouldn't be this upset. But I am. I'm mad at myself for letting him back into my life. Angry that I put myself through this all over again against my better judgement. But most of all, it's my already broken heart that aches. I didn't think it could break anymore, but each jagged shard snaps in two.

My phone chimes, but I don't bother looking at it. I can't even bring myself to reach for it.

Someone buzzes the door, but I ignore it. It's probably some delivery person trying to drop off greasy burgers for hungover customers, pushing every button until they get let in.

Felix hops on the bed, sitting at the edge, watching me with curious eyes the longer the door buzzes. He's not that concerned, grooming his paws, pausing with his tongue out when the door buzzes again.

I'm grateful for the distraction. The buzzing is enough for me to focus on stopping the tears, and Felix's judgmental gaze is more than enough motivation to pull myself together.

I breathe deeply, letting it out slowly through pursed lips. My palms press against my swollen eyes as a barrier for the wayward tears that refuse to stop falling.

But what really stops them is a fierce pounding on the door.

Felix leaps off the bed with lightning speed. I jackknife up, heart racing at the unexpected interruption. "What the fuck?"

I creep on tiptoes out of my bedroom, peeking my head into the living room.

The door rattles again, the knocking insistent. A familiar, muffled voice comes from the other side. "Dani? Open the door."

And damn it, hearing Logan's voice acts like a soothing balm.

With one last swipe of my cheeks, I open the door. "How did you even get in?"

"Mrs. Humphry." Those dark eyes don't miss a thing. They zero in on my puffy eyes and red cheeks. "What happened?"

I can't go around telling him I'm having a mental breakdown because of him. Right?

I turn on my heel, letting him let himself in so I can figure out how the hell I'm going to dodge his questions. "Mean old lady Humphry?"

"She likes me." I hear more than see his shrug. "Dani."

Cold leather creaks underneath me. "Logan."

He stands in front of the fireplace watching me with a critical gaze. I can't stand it.

"How was the cabin? Did Miles get a few punches in?"

Logan's hair is ruffled, his shirt wrinkled, hands resting on his hip. His brow furrows in confusion. I know he won't let this go, but he humors me. "He got his revenge. Cooper beat me to the couch, so I had to sleep on the floor."

"Explains the bags under your eyes."

He doesn't take the bait. "Were you crying?"

Why is he being so attentive? Tears gather in my eyes. "No." A lone tear spills over, and I wipe it away. Maybe he didn't notice.

Of course he does.

In two long strides, Logan sits next to me, arms wrapping around me. "Dani."

The way he says my name, so soft, reopens the floodgates.

"I'm fine," I say through thick vocal cords. "It's nothing."

"I'm sure you are. But tell me anyway." A finger brushes along my cheek.

For several moments, Logan sits with me, never letting me go, thumbs stroking comfortingly on my thigh. Waiting.

Maybe it's the way he's offering me strength. Maybe it's the soft way he's holding me, but I want to tell him. I want to show him how he hurt me.

My breath catches in my throat. "When Robbie died, and you left," I swallow. "It...left its mark."

He inhales sharply through his nose, nodding slowly.

"It hit me that you're about to leave again." I fiddle with my shirtsleeve, unable to look at him.

Sharing my feelings with someone isn't easy.

"Dani." His voice is soft, and it makes more tears well. A warm palm cups my face, turning me to look at him. I don't want to, but I look anyway.

Home.

That's what I feel when I look into his brown eyes, but I know it's only temporary.

Because it won't last.

He'll still leave. Head out the door and never come back.

I can't take it. Breathe fills my lungs as I steel my spine, and look away from him. Break away from the intense look in his eyes, because if I dared to linger, it would show how wrong I am.

But I don't.

I can't.

"Dani," he says again, more pleading and desperate. "I'm not leaving." He ignores my scoff. "I mean, I have to go back, but I'm not staying gone. You need to know that."

It's the same thing he's been saying since Christmas Eve, but I can't believe him.

Because if I do, I know I'll splinter into a thousand pieces when he makes a fool of me.

"I never thought you would leave the first time either." The anger that seemed to dissolve when he showed up at my door rears its ugly head. "You left me alone." I look at him. "I was alone," my voice breaks. "You don't get to come back into my life, flip it upside down, and leave again." I shake my head. "I'm such an idiot."

Logan hangs his head. "I'm the idiot."

A laugh bubbles up my throat. "You won't hear any argument from me."

He stands. "Will you listen to me for once instead of thinking of what to say next?" Logan's not shouting, but the tone of his voice has me frozen.

The room falls quiet, Logan's pacing feet on hardwood the only sound.

After several minutes, I clear my throat. "This is me shutting up."

A humorless laugh huffs from him. "Thanks for the update."

Felix hops into my lap, purr already rumbling. My anger boiled over and has returned to a simmer. The tears that were once free-flowing have dried.

"I fucked up. I know that. And I'm sorry for leaving you." His throat bobs. "I was selfish and weak, so I left. It killed me every day to know that I let you down, let everyone down." His voice wavers with emotion, tears brimming in his eyes. "I fucked up."

I want to roll my eyes and make a jabbing response, but what good would it do? It might make me feel better in the moment, but it would only hurt us both in the end.

Instead, I do as he asked, listening and processing his words.

We're just two broken people barely hanging on. I may not have run away, but I've been just as weak, just as selfish. Haven't I pushed Lindsay away? Holed myself up in this mausoleum of an apartment with reminders of my dead family around every corner. Refused to show up for a single Christmas when I know it gets rough for her too.

Am I being selfish, even right now? Yes, he messed up. Yes, he abandoned me.

But he also came back.

That has to mean something, right?

"But how do I know you won't do it again? I won't be the stupid girl that believes the guy because he gives a half-hearted attempt at an apology." Even though I want to believe him. So badly.

Desperation. It's etched into every line of his face, the rise and fall of his chest, resting in the depths of his brown eyes. He rakes a hand down his face. "What do you want me to say, Dani?"

I toss my hands up, frustrated at everything. "I don't know." Part of me wants him to grab me in a hug, holding me so tight I can't breathe. Tell me over and over again that he won't leave until I believe him. Kiss me so intensely that I forget about everything.

Logan plops onto the couch next to me, head in his hands. "You mean so much to me," he breathes. "You're all I think about. The whole time I was with my brothers, all I could picture was how beautiful you were when I left the apartment. That having to leave you for one night was almost unbearable." He huffs a laugh. "I dragged Cooper off the couch first thing this morning because I couldn't stand to be away from you for one more minute. When you didn't answer your phone or the damn door, I buzzed your neighbor. You've crawled under my skin, Dani." His eyes meet mine. "If I wasn't blind back then, I would've seen how much I need you. You've brought back the man I never thought I'd be again. So, no, Dani. I'm not leaving again, because I can't."

And damn it if those aren't the words I wanted to hear.

The earnestness of his voice, the pleading, desperate look in his eyes...it's working. I want to believe him. I need to believe him, because I can't face the alternative. It might be foolish of me. He could be giving lip service and nothing more. But...

"You promise?" My voice is as shaky as a newborn fawn. I'm practically vibrating with uncertainty, but believing him also feels *right*.

Logan watches me, his eyes bouncing around my face, taking in every minute expression. Slowly, he leans in, every move deliberate, giving me the chance to say no. Gentle as a feather caressing skin, Logan kisses me. "I promise."

Chapter Ten

Logan
One Month Later

"Lift it."

"I swear to God, Logan, I am!" Allison whines from the other side of the couch we're hauling to my new apartment.

Having my baby sister help wasn't the best idea, but it's not like I could stop her. She's too damn hardheaded. Once she got the information out of me, which wasn't that hard, she had already cleared her schedule.

"We're almost there. Just...lift."

"I don't know how Dani puts up with you," she mutters.

A cocky smile pulls at my lips. "I make up for it in other ways."

"Ew, gross."

Even though we've been apart for the last month, our video calls weren't always innocent. Images of her hand drifting low between her thighs, her teeth sinking into that juicy bottom lip as she...

No, can't be sprinting down that rabbit hole.

Just a couple more hours.

Allison complains the entire way to the apartment. I would've had one of my brother's help, but me being back is a secret—one only Allison decoded.

Before I left Chicago, I was already plotting to move back. Our short time together changed everything.

Changed me.

It wasn't a hard decision. I need to be close to my family. To her. The logistics of making it all happen took some time. Finding an apartment, transferring back to the Chicago office, and now secretly moving in before Dani knows I'm back. That's been the hardest part.

Every muscle twitches with the need to see her. Hold her. To simply be in the same room as her.

Something swirls in my chest. Anticipation flows down my spine, through my fingers and toes. Nothing's ever felt more right, and I can't wait to tell her.

Allison braces her hands on her knees trying to catch her breath. "Why do you have so much stuff?"

I scoff. "Did you forget all the shit we moved into your dorm room? Two truckloads for that tiny room."

She straightens, pointing a defensive finger. "I needed it all."

I plop onto the couch. "And I need this."

My sister surveys the room before sitting next to me. "So, what's the plan?"

Boxes and bags litter the floor. "Um, get my things unpacked."

She clicks her tongue. "No, dummy. What's your plan for Dani?"

"Other than surprising her early?" I shrug. I hadn't thought past seeing her in person, getting to hold her, talking to her.

I miss her more than I've missed anyone—except for Robbie. I miss him every day.

But Dani?

I miss her *presence.*

Most nights, I wake from dreams of her in my arms to cold sheets. I miss the sound of her snorts when she sees something funny. How she rolls her eyes when she thinks I'm being dumb. The soft way she talks to Felix. Watching her in the mirror when she gets ready to leave the house. Small moments that get lost in the daily shuffle. Things that can't be seen through a phone screen. Those are the things I miss.

"You need a plan." She taps her chin, a crooked smile tugging at her lips.

I know that look. It's the one that usually means I'm going to have to do something I don't want to. "And I'm assuming you have one?" I sigh.

Her smile is mischievous. "Maybe."

"Tell me while we work."

DAMN MY LITTLE SISTER. Apparently, I have a weakness for stubborn women, because I keep finding myself in these insane situations.

But once Allison gets an idea in her head, she won't let go. Like a buzzing bee, Allison concocted a plan and flew out the door before I had the chance to object. So here I am. I can picture her smug face, delighted that everything's going according to plan.

Chicago in February is the same as it's always been. Sirens echo through the city streets. A light breeze crinkles the cellophane in my hand. The cool air fills my lungs, doing nothing to calm my racing heart.

It's been a month since I've walked this sidewalk, only this time, I'm more nervous than the last time I did this. There's more riding on this than I want to admit. The last time was a lot, but now?

Last time, I had something to gain. Now, I have something to lose. I can't let that happen.

My phone call with Dani earlier was quick. It's become a routine that I look forward to, but tonight I had different motives. It was more difficult than I expected to keep another secret from her, but under Allison's watchful eyes, I let nothing slip.

The light from her apartment radiates through her window. I can picture her lying on the couch after a long day of work, a purring Felix on her chest while she chomps through a bag of chips. I chuckle at the thought, because that's what she was doing when I called her.

Dani's apartment key slips into my palm. I'm sure when she gave this to me before I left she didn't think I would use it to surprise her. *'Emergency situations'* is what she said when she placed it in my palm.

Too bad she wasn't specific about what an emergency is. Because it feels pretty damn urgent to see her.

Standing at the bottom of the steps, I suck in a breath, letting it out slowly.

Here goes nothing.

There's no holding back my excitement. I take the stairs two at a time, and when I reach her door, I'm winded.

She's right behind this door. I'll be able to hold her in my arms in a matter of moments.

With a steady hand, I knock.

My heart pounds; my palms sweat. Hell, I'm sure sweat is beading on my forehead. I don't think I've been this nervous about something, well, since the last time I showed up here hoping and praying that she answers the door.

I rock back on my heels, anticipation building.

C'mon, Dani. Open the door.

I knock again, louder this time.

"C'mon, c'mon, c'mon." I could use the key that feels like a lead weight in my pocket, but I won't. She's more likely to beat me with a skillet for scaring the shit out of her than be happy to see me.

Just as I'm about to lift my fist, the door whooshes open. I barely have time to mutter a word before Dani is in my arms.

Legs wrap around my waist; soft hair tickles my nose.

Dani.

The flowers in my hand fall to the floor as I grab her and hold her close.

Eyes squeezed tight, I breathe her in. It's like I haven't breathed in months. I've been suffocating and didn't notice until this moment.

"How are you here?" she mutters against my neck before pulling back to look at me.

Hair falls in her face, and I brush it away. "I came back early. To surprise you."

Heavy tears slip down her cheeks. She smiles. "You came back."

"Of course I did." I cup her face. "I told you I would."

She huffs a laugh. "Yeah, well, I wouldn't—"

I drag her lips to mine. It's been too long since I've tasted her, and I can't wait one more second.

Dani moans, hands fisting in my hair. She opens to me, tongues flicking and teasing.

Plastic crunches under my feet as I move through her open doorway. I'll have to come back for the squished flowers. Right now, Dani is all I care about.

I move us through the kitchen, setting her on the counter, our kiss never breaking. Our hands roam as if neither of us quite believe the other is here. The curve of her hips, the swell of her breasts, the soft column of her neck. I've been dreaming of her in my arms, and now it's finally a reality.

"Hi," I breathe, once we pull apart.

Dani smiles, her hazel eyes sparkling. "Hi."

For a moment, I'm lost in the depths of her eyes and the light shining from them. Gone are the dark circles that used to rest beneath them. Sadness no longer lives on the surface, etched in every flicker of movement. It's still there, never quite leaving, but overshadowed with life and happiness.

I kiss her. "I missed you. So much."

Her brows arch. "So much that you lied to me and showed up at my door a day early?"

My hands rest on her hips. "You know, some would say that it's not lying if it's for a surprise."

She shrugs, placing her arms on my shoulders. "And the suit?"

I snicker. "Allison's idea." I step back, letting her examine the black velvet suit.

"You look nice. It's much better than the Santa suit, I'll give you that." Her eyes trail over my shoulders before slipping down my torso. She might hide it, but I can see how much she likes it. She reaches for me, her palms running down the velvet lapels before tugging on them, bringing me back to her.

"That suit isn't going anywhere. In fact, I think I'll have to buy one."

Dani rolls her eyes. "I missed you, too."

I press our foreheads together. My mouth works with the words I've been wanting to say, but nothing comes out.

A trill of a meow follows the faint thud of feet on the counter. Felix's gray head nudges my arm before he rubs against Dani's back. "I think he missed you too," she laughs.

"I doubt it. He only thinks he missed me. Give him a couple of days, and he'll be back to glaring at me from across the room."

Dani pulls back, her hands slipping away to pet Felix. "Don't listen to him, Felix. He doesn't know you like I do. I know you missed him."

As quickly as he appeared, Felix leaves us with a swish of his tail. "Yeah, he was distraught."

"Completely beside himself."

She's so beautiful smiling up at me I can't stop the words. "I love you."

Dani freezes. The sudden deep breaths are the only clue that she heard me.

The longer the silence drags, the more panic swells in my chest. The words are out, and I can't take them back.

I'm in love with my best friend's sister, and she might not love me back. I could've just ruined the most important relationship I have left. "Can you—"

Fingers press against my lips. "Hold on." Dani's wide eyes blink, her mouth parting ever so slightly. "You need to tell me exactly what you mean, because I'm not convinced I heard you correctly."

My hands squeeze her hips. "I love you, Dani. I've always loved you, but this is different. I'm *in* love with you. Ever since I came back to Chicago, things have changed. Having you back in my life changed me. Holding you, kissing you, being with you is something I never saw coming, but now that I have it, I can't let you go. I don't want to let you go. And I know Robbie would kill me for it, but I love you."

"You...love me?"

I brush hair away from her face. "Yes, Dani. I love you."

"Are you sure? Because if you're kidding, Logan Miller, I swear to God—"

This time, I'm the one shutting her up with a kiss. I melt into her, pouring all the love that's been building in my chest into it. She's no longer frozen, her arms wrapping around me and pulling me closer to her. This kiss is laced with more than desperate longing. It's filled with something too intense to put a name to.

"I love you," I whisper against her lips. "And I plan on saying it every day for the rest of our lives."

She smiles. "I'm glad you finally came around."

I jolt back, peering at her bright face. "What?"

Dani kisses me. "Logan, I was in love with you before you left." Hands brush through my hair. "I didn't want to admit it to myself because I was scared I was going to lose you. But I do. I love you."

My eyes drift closed as the words settle in my chest.

She loves me. I've fucked up in so many ways, made so many mistakes, but right now? I finally got something right. Because she loves me. She's seen my flaws, my sorrow, and she let me back into her life. Back into her heart.

Robbie died, and the world as I knew it fell apart. *Our* world fell apart. I just didn't know how much we needed each other. Maybe this was always meant to be. Perhaps it's Robbie, doing one last thing for the people he loves from beyond the grave.

Dani squeals when I lift her off the counter. "Logan, what are you doing?"

I smack her ass. "I just told the woman I love I love her. Now, it's time to show her."

She snickers. "So that's what this is all about. You just want sex."

"Dani, I've been away from you for a fucking month. Of course, I want to have sex with you. But you just told me you love me, and I don't think I can keep my hands off of you."

"Hm, I don't know. You seem pretty tame to me." Her eyes sparkle down at me, a teasing smile on her lips.

I can't wait to wipe it off her face.

Epilogue

Danielle
Five Months Later

C emeteries are kind of peaceful. Still creepy, but not in the 'zombies are attacking through a mist-covered gravesite' way movies always make them out to be.

They're quiet. Still.

A place to think. To grieve. Remember.

Sunlight filters through the tree leaves, shading us as I lead Logan through the cemetery. Strong fingers grip mine, the only outward sign that he's nervous.

Convincing him to come with me wasn't hard. Logan's worked through a lot of his grief, and thanks to him, so have I. We're nowhere near perfect; we still have bad days, but now I can think about my parents and brother with a fondness not tainted by hollow grief.

But this is hard.

Especially today.

Four years ago today, Robbie died.

Four years ago, life as I knew it ceased to exist for the second time.

I inhale a hitching breath, letting it out slowly through pursed lips. The air smells of summer warmth and stargazer lilies, their scent wafting up from the bundle clutched in my fist. They were Mom's favorite. The flower shop didn't have the orange ones that she liked, but I don't think she'd mind the pale pink ones currently bouncing in the breeze.

I spot Robbie's grave. easily. There were no funeral plans to follow when he died. No place for him next to Mom and Dad in the mausoleum. No one to help me decide what to do.

It still hurts knowing that I was alone. That I had to deal with my brother's death alone. That I had to pick the bronze plaque in place of a granite stone.

Logan must sense the direction of my thoughts, his hand squeezing mine. "You okay?"

I swallow back the lump in my throat. "I'll be fine." My footsteps slow, waiting for him to match my pace. I kiss his shoulder before resting my head against it. "Are you okay?"

He's quiet for a moment. "No. I don't think I am. But I will be."

We maneuver through the maze of headstones, coming to a stop in front of Robbie's. Logan loosens his grip on my hand, and I kneel, wiping off dirt and dust. I didn't bother bringing flowers for Robbie—he hated them. But I brought something else.

My bag slips off my shoulder, the familiar clank of aluminum rattling together. I grab the cold can, popping the beer open with a whoosh and a click. "Couldn't show up without your favorite." The can clinks against the bronze plaque, the bubbles hissing. "Here." I stand, holding out the other can. "I thought you guys would like to have a drink."

Logan's eyes are heavy with unshed tears. He nods, taking the can and cracking it open. I place a hand on his chest before kissing him. "I'm gonna go see my parents."

He nods, and I let my hand slip off his chest as I walk away.

I've had my time to sit at my brother's grave. So many words have drifted in the wind here. Tears have soaked into the hard dirt. One-sided conversations that are more for myself than the dead.

That's what Logan needs. He needs time with his best friend.

I sniff, wiping away the lone tear that threatens to spill down my cheeks.

The polished granite building looms in the distance, surrounded by blooming trees, their purplish-pink flowers beautiful in the sunlight. Family members visit their relatives throughout the sprawling cemetery, each with heads bowed, gazing at the grave of their loved one.

No one's in the mausoleum. The sudden chill makes me shiver. Gold nameplates line the walls, showing the final resting place of the person behind them.

The atmosphere here is different. Heavier than the lightness of the open air outside.

My eyes scan the walls as I pass, reading name after name until I see my parents. "I brought you flowers." Plastic crinkles as I remove the layer protecting the flowers and place them in the vase between their plaques.

I sit on a nearby bench, lost in memories.

My parents have always been hard for me to recall. I can picture their faces, hear their voices. But I can only catch bits and pieces of the thirteen years I had with them.

Dad loved his muscle cars. He and Robbie spent many Sunday evenings under the hood of a car coming in smelling like grease and sweat. I laugh as a memory of Dad wrapping his greasy hands around Mom's waist, both of them laughing as he kissed her.

Mom's memories are quieter. Her sitting under a lamp late at night crocheting. Coming inside with dirt-covered gloves after working in the flower beds.

The longer I sit, the more memories flood my vision. I lose track of time in them, my eyes slipping closed, watching the flashes of them pass like trees through a car window. Quick glimpses filled with happiness tinged with sadness.

My legs tingle from sitting still for so long. I stand on shaky legs, kissing my fingers and placing them on the cold granite before walking away. There are no words to say, just the quiet admiration for the people they were.

Logan's sitting where I left him, arms resting on his knees. The beer can dangles between his hands in a loose grip. He watches me make my way to him, patting the ground next to him.

I nudge his shoulder. "Enjoying your drink?"

He laughs, but his eyes are red from tears. He shakes the empty can. "All gone."

"I don't think Robbie would mind if you drank his." I wrap my arm through his and lean my head against his shoulder.

"Nah. He deserves every last drop." He kisses the top of my head. "How was seeing your parents?"

I sigh. "It was good. Quiet." He hums. "Well, Robbie, looks like the cats outta the bag. How do you feel about your little sister and your best friend falling in love?"

Logan chuckles. "He's taking it rather well, I'd say."

"And how are you taking it?"

He's quiet for a minute, his gaze lingering straight ahead. I stare at his profile, watching the tick of his jaw as he gathers his thoughts. "It's, uh," he clears his throat, "I think I'm okay."

"Yeah?"

"I don't remember the last words I said to him." His admission hangs between us. "But I think I've realized that it doesn't matter. He knew I loved him, even if I didn't say it. But, God, I miss him. So much."

The tears I've been waiting for finally fall. They soak into the fabric of his shirt, but Logan's too busy wiping away his own to notice. "I miss him, too."

He sniffles, a chuckle sneaking from his throat. "I bet he'd be happy to know we think about him so much. The asshole loved being the center of attention."

"He did," I laugh.

We fall silent, letting the tears dry.

Logan kisses the top of my head. "You ready to go?"

"Only if you are."

Logan's brown eyes meet mine, filled with so much emotion that it steals my breath. The man I love has a clear gaze for the first time since he's come back. So much pain and sorrow rested behind those brown eyes, and now it's replaced with a serene calm. "I love you."

Scruff rubs against the palm I place on his cheek. "I love you."

Logan kisses me, sending the world spinning around us. "Let's go home."

Thanks For Reading

I hope you enjoyed reading *Eggnog and Whiskey*.

I f you could, please take a moment to rate and review on Amazon, Goodreads, Instagram, or wherever you post reviews. As an indie author, ratings and reviews are the best way of getting my work out there for other people to read.

A little goes a long way!

Until next tine,

Sierra

About the Author

S ierra Shipley is a born and raised Midwest girl. She spends her days with her lovable rescue pup, Trip, who constantly wants all the cuddles, and her lovable cat Aidas. Her ideal day is spent drinking coffee, reading, and dreaming.

Sierra has always wanted the romance she's read in books. Pair that with an active imagination and a love of creativity, and you get a writer!

Sierra wants to create steamy, romantic stories with characters that people can relate to.

www.ingramcontent.com/pod-product-compliance
Lightning Source LLC
Chambersburg PA
CBHW030355180626
46812CB00007B/2899